Christmas in heaven: what an image of the best Christmas ever! Only a little child—and Phyllis Clark Nichols—could lead us there.

—DIANE KOMP, MD
PROFESSOR OF PEDIATRICS EMERITUS
YALE SCHOOL OF MEDICINE
AUTHOR OF THE BEST-SELLING *A WINDOW TO HEAVEN*
AND *THE HEALER'S HEART*

This uplifting tale by my dear friend Phyllis Clark Nichols will, I hope, warm hearts and give faith at Christmastime.

—ABRAHAM VERGHESE, MD
VICE CHAIR FOR THE THEORY AND PRACTICE OF
MEDICINE, STANFORD UNIVERSITY
BEST-SELLING AUTHOR OF *CUTTING FOR STONE*
THE TENNIS PARTNER, AND *MY OWN COUNTRY*

One of life's greatest tragedies is when a young person is forced to endure the loss of a parent. In *The Christmas Portrait* Phyllis Clark Nichols gives us a heartwarming glimpse into the mind and life of a young girl who must make this painful transition. The story of how she manages to find her way through the sorrow and emerge with a strengthened faith in God and family is both fulfilling and emotional. This really is a remarkable book, one that challenges the reader to make each moment in life count and to work each day to bring a smile to someone's face

Life is complicat‗‗‗‗‗‗‗‗‗‗‗‗‗‗‗‗‗ ‑at compete for our time ‗‗‗‗‗‗‗‗‗‗‗‗‗‗‗‗‗ *las Portrait* Phyllis Clark‗‗‗‗‗‗‗‗‗‗‗‗‗‗‗‗‗ pause and consider what‗‗‗‗‗‗‗‗‗‗‗‗‗‗‗‗‗ friends, faith, and yes, contentment. ‗‗‗‗‗‗‗‗‗‗‗‗ ‗h about

how powerful this story is and how well written. I highly recommend it. Read it. And then read it again.

—BILL AIRY
CHIEF STRATEGY OFFICER
LeSEA BROADCASTING CORPORATION

A story of family, love, loss, and faith through the eyes of a child. It's a good read for any season of the year, not just Christmas. The author has developed her characters well, which helps us "feel" the time, place, and depth of the story.

—DONALD L. ANDERSON, PhD
MINISTER AND PSYCHOLOGIST
EXECUTIVE DIRECTOR EMERITUS,
ECUMENICAL CENTER FOR RELIGION AND HEALTH

The Christmas Portrait is a masterful work of storytelling that artfully blends the hues of realism and hope. In this artfully poignant story of emotional healing, Phyllis Clark Nichols opens our spirits to comprehend how mysteriously God speaks through a bird, a portrait, a profound loss, and a desperate act of love. This story has real lift, a buoyant hope that begins in Christmas and ends wherever the reader will let it take them.

For all those who find unwanted loss and grief under their Christmas tree, here is a story of hope rising through the tenacious love of a heartbroken child and the mysterious relationships she opens herself up to.

—BRAD RUSSELL, DMin
FOUNDER AND SENIOR EDITOR
FAITHVILLAGE.COM

Written in the register of love and longing *The Christmas Portrait* invites the reader to enter the story of a grieving family through the eyes of a ten-year-old girl, Kate. The carefully wrought narrative portrays the power of faith, thick family bonds, and a sense of place in the wooded hills of northern Kentucky. With sensitivity to the holy revealed through nature and a mysterious visitor—an angel perhaps?—the author weaves a story of renewal as Kate and her family find ways to celebrate their love of her mother while becoming open to the ever-moving stream that is life. I commend the book for its shimmering beauty, its perceptive wisdom about human brokenness, and its unyielding faith in the promise of the future.

—Dr. Molly Marshall
President, Central Baptist Theological Seminary

The Christmas Portrait is a gift well timed for today's restless readership. I loved it and celebrated the reasonableness of Christmas joy applied to the everyday of its timeless adventure. The accuracy of its storytelling allows the reader to participate in the reality of a joyous Christmas and to claim comforting kinship with its fellowship of joy.

—Jeannette Clift George
Actress known for her portrayal of
Corrie ten Boom in *The Hiding Place*

The Christmas

PORTRAIT

Phyllis Clark Nichols

REALMS

Most CHARISMA HOUSE BOOK GROUP products are available at special quantity discounts for bulk purchase for sales promotions, premiums, fund-raising, and educational needs. For details, write Charisma House Book Group, 600 Rinehart Road, Lake Mary, Florida 32746, or telephone (407) 333-0600.

THE CHRISTMAS PORTRAIT by Phyllis Clark Nichols
Published by Realms
Charisma Media/Charisma House Book Group
600 Rinehart Road
Lake Mary, Florida 32746
www.charismahouse.com

All Scripture quotations are from the King James Version of the Bible; Holy Bible, New International Version, Copyright © 1973, 1978, 1984, International Bible Society; New American Standard Bible, copyright © 1960, 1962, 1963, 1968, 1971, 1972, 1973, 1975, 1977, 1995 by The Lockman Foundation, (www.Lockman.org). All versions are used by permission.

Cover Design by Lisa Rae McClure
Design Director: Justin Evans

Visit the author's website at www.phyllisclarknichols.com.

Library of Congress Cataloging-in-Publication Data:
Nichols, Phyllis Clark.
  The Christmas portrait / by Phyllis Clark Nichols. -- First
edition.
      pages cm
  ISBN 978-1-62998-216-8 (trade paper) -- ISBN 978-1-
62998-217-5 (e-book)
  1. Bereavement in children--Religious aspects--Christianity.
2. Children and death--Religious aspects--Christianity. 3.
Harding, Katherine Joy. 4. Harding John Chesler--Family. 5.
Mothers--Death. I. Title.
  BV4596.P3N53 2015
  248.8'66083--dc23

                                          2015025279

First edition

15 16 17 18 19 — 987654321
Printed in the United States of America

*For Mama, Aunt Marguerite,
and Katy Piper*

ACKNOWLEDGMENTS

A WRITER NEEDS A reader. So thank you for reading my book. Just as printed music on a conductor's score becomes real music when played by the orchestra or intoned by the choir, this story comes to life as it is read. Thousands of words are only ink on pages until someone opens the cover and starts to read. It is then that characters speak and scenes take on color and dimension. Thank you for taking a few hours of your life to read this story. These are hours you cannot recapture. My prayer is that you will find an idea, a phrase, or a nugget of truth that you will remember when you need it.

A writer needs a story. I am deeply indebted to three women whom I have loved dearly and who have had tremendous influence on my life: my own mother, Betty Clark; my Aunt Marguerite Lewis; and my dear friend Katy Piper. These women all lost their mothers when they were very young, and yet they have mothered me in immeasurable ways and taught me important life lessons. Their lives gave me the story and the desire to write it. Then there were all the beautiful Christmases of my growing up years that made this story easy to write. Thank you, Mama and Daddy.

A writer needs good ideas. A few years ago while at a retreat at Laity Lodge out in the Texas Hill Country,

I was challenged by Dr. Dave Peterson, a Presbyterian minister, to choose something tangible that would remind me of God's presence and activity in my life. I quickly identified that crimson flicker of life we call a cardinal as my "God-alert." Since then I have grown plants and provided their favorite treats to entice them to my garden. I am indebted to Dr. Peterson for this concept, which has encouraged me to practice God's presence and for the idea it gave me for this story.

A writer needs encouragement. I offer deep gratitude to my dear friend, Dr. Abraham Verghese, a most gifted writer and physician, who said to me, "If there's a book in you, then write it." He marked and stacked books from his own library to illustrate what he was teaching me and sent me to the bookstore with instructions not to leave until I had pulled forty books from the shelves and read the first paragraphs of each of them.

I am grateful to friends who endorsed this work and to others who have encouraged my creativity: Deb Cleveland held me accountable with her calls and conversations about the writing process; Letha Crouch and Camille Simmons inspired me with their own creativity; Blanche Armendariz, Jimmy and Shirley Elrod, Lottie Mitchell, Dr. David Shacklett, Susan Chastain, and Janie Jones read my words and told me to keep writing.

A writer needs a champion. I will never be able to thank my agent, Mary Beth Chappell Lyle, enough for believing in my work, for guiding me, and for pushing me to be better. She was my first editor. Her porcelain skin covers a tender heart, and she speaks with the gentility of a Southern woman, but she is tough-minded, tenacious, and committed to excellence. Without her, I'd still be wandering around wondering if I can write.

I would also like to thank my new friends at Charisma House. Thank you, Adrienne Gaines, for your belief in this book and for always being there with answers when I called. This book is immeasurably better because of the meticulous reads and the thoughtful suggestions of Lori Vandenbosh, my editor. Thank you for pushing me to see how committed I was, Lori.

A writer needs a hand to hold and solitude. My husband, Bill, holds my hand always—sometimes because we just like to hold hands; sometimes to pull me along; sometimes to lead me away from the safe, comfortable places to the edge of new ideas; and sometimes to take me on long walks through these hills where we enjoy each other and the beauty of God's creation. What a gift to have a husband who is a philosopher, theologian, and artist! My hours and days are rich with him. He also provided the solitude, protecting my time, manning the doorbell and the phone, and graciously declining invitations when needed. I wouldn't say he mastered laundry or meal preparation, but he knows what every button on the microwave does, and he was always willing. Without Bill's handholding and encouragement, this book would not be a reality.

And I am most thankful to my Father, the author of life, for instilling in me the desire to write stories. His parables not only teach us the truth of living life His way, they show us what He thinks about the power of the narrative. And I thank Him for the redbirds who sat in the feeder at my window as I wrote. I am grateful to Him for what I know about *faith, family, and forever.*

PROLOGUE

Chicago
December 2006

R. KATE, DO they have Christmas in heaven?" Marla sat across the table from me. She held tightly to as many crayons as she could hold in her petite left hand and colored with her right.

"Now that's a very interesting question. Do you have a reason for asking?" I continued sketching, not giving any hint of my surprise at her inquiry.

"Well, my sister wanted this pretty necklace for Christmas. She showed it to me in the store window, and she wanted it real bad. But that man in the blue truck ran over her, and now she's in heaven." Her crayon never left the page while she spoke. A Christmas tree, donned with a yellow butterfly tree topper, was taking shape on her page.

I laid my drawing pencil down, propped my elbows on the table, and leaned forward. "That's a good question, Marla. What do you think?"

"I think there's Christmas in heaven." She never looked at me.

"I think so too. In fact, I think heaven may be like having Christmas every day."

She continued to color. "That's good. That means Abby likes it. Maybe I could go there too."

"I'm sure Abby likes it there, but for now, don't you want to stay here with your family?"

"Uh-huh, but I want to see Abby too."

"I know you want to see your big sister." I looked at her work, picked up my pencil, and started to sketch again. A likeness was appearing. "You're using all the bright Christmas colors today. That makes me so happy. Do they make you happy too?"

"I don't know. I just like red and green and blue and yellow."

"So do I."

"But you're not coloring. You're just drawing. Why don't you use colors like me?" She handed me the red crayon. "Here, you need this one."

"Thank you, Marla." I took the crayon and twirled it through the fingers of my left hand. "I'm just doodling while we talk."

"Do you just sit here and doodle all day, Dr. Kate?"

How purely delightful that sounded. "You're just full of good questions today. I do get to draw sometimes, but mostly what I do is sit and listen and talk to people. I help them draw and color and make things so they'll feel better."

"That sounds like a fun job. Is that why I have to call you doctor, because you make people feel better?"

"Well, I guess it is. Would it be okay if I ask you a question, Marla?"

"Uh-huh. I mean, yes, ma'am."

"What's on your Christmas list this year?"

"I just mostly want my sister back, and I want my mommy not to cry at nighttime." Marla stopped coloring and searched through the box of crayons. She chose the black one and started to scribble a jagged black border around her Christmas tree.

"You know, that sounds a lot like what your mommy wants for Christmas too. She wants you not to be so sad. That's why she brings you here to talk to me. Is there anything else on your list, like a doll, or maybe you'd like a necklace too?"

"Nope, I just want my sister back and my mommy not to be so sad. There's nobody to sleep in my sister's bed."

I put my hand on hers and removed her crayon. "Marla, look at me, sweetie. I know this is your first Christmas without your sister, and it will be different. Do you know how I know that?"

She looked at me as though I were about to tell her the biggest secret she'd ever heard. "Because you're a doctor and you know things?"

"No. I know because I was just like you. When I was ten, my mother died, and I missed her so much, especially at Christmas. It was very hard, but everything turned out all right."

I couldn't tell her that when Mama died that late September night she left a vacuum that sucked the life and color right out of my world. Overnight, the trees dressed in red and gold were only naked limbs, and the mountains on the horizon looked like chiseled gray stone pasted against a gray sky. The days became chilly and ushered in the coldest, snowiest winter on record in northern Kentucky. Even the earth mourned the loss of Mama.

"Do you still miss your mommy?"

"I do miss her. But now, I'm not so sad anymore. I'm just grateful she was my mother, and I'll never forget her. She's the one who taught me to draw, and she's the one who taught me my job in life is to try to make people happy. She'll always be with me because of my memories."

I could tell her the days grew warm again even if it seemed forever. And the trees budded and the mountains turned green, but walking those mountain paths wasn't the same. No more holding Mama's hand or singing her silly songs. When the colors finally returned, I saw them differently. I could explain this to Marla. I just wish I could believe it for her. Only the passing of days would make her believe.

I asked Marla, "Don't you remember how we've talked about your memories of Abby?"

She nodded in agreement. "At home I tried to draw a picture about the time we went camping, and she caught the biggest fish."

"That's good. That's really good, Marla. You keep drawing those pictures. Would you do something else for me?"

She looked up at me. "Sure."

"I want you to put something on your Christmas list that Santa can put under your tree. I think that'll make you smile big on Christmas morning. Would you do that?"

"Yes, ma'am. I already know what it is."

"That's good, and you be sure to tell your mom what it is. In fact, our time's almost up, and she's probably out front waiting on us."

Marla slid her drawing into the yellow plastic pouch and started putting her crayons in the wooden box, lining them up neatly. I stood to help her.

"May I see what you're drawing, Dr. Kate?"

"Certainly, it's not finished though." I slid my sketch pad across the table.

She looked at the drawing and then at me. "See, I knew you needed the red crayon. You like redbirds, don't you?"

"As a matter of fact, I do."

"I thought so. They're everywhere around here." Her eyes surveyed the room from her three-foot vantage spot.

I took her hand, and we walked toward the lobby. "You know how you chose the yellow butterfly to help you remember your sister? And we talked about how Abby was like a beautiful butterfly coming out of a cocoon and how she's free now."

"Uh-huh, I remember. I draw yellow butterflies in all my pictures. I drew one today. It was on top of the Christmas tree." She was swinging her arm and mine as we walked hand in hand through the studio. It was the first carefree, childlike body language I had seen since I met her a few weeks ago.

"That's good. Just keep drawing those yellow butterflies, and I'll draw redbirds because it helps me remember my mother. She had red hair, and she could sing like a song-bird." We entered the front office.

"There's a redbird!" Marla pointed to the embroidered bird in the center of the memory quilt hanging on the wall next to the door. "And there's another one!" She pointed to the grouping of pictures above the sofa. "Did you take that picture?"

"I did. I took that picture with my very first camera. The redbird was right outside our living room window."

"Wow! I'd like to take a picture of a butterfly."

"Maybe you can someday."

Marla nearly lunged toward the sofa, and climbed up on both knees. She leaned close to see. "Dr. Kate, do you know him too?"

"Who, Marla?"

"Him." Her eyes were fixed on the framed picture next to the redbird.

Her words halted my movement. I replayed them in my head. Do you know him too?

"You mean the man in that portrait I painted?"

"Uh-huh. Him." She pointed to the picture and then looked at me.

"Yes. I met him a long time ago. Why? Do you know Mr. Josh?"

She turned around and sat down on the sofa. "I sort of know him. He was at the butterfly haven the other day, and he talked to me about missing Abby."

"Did he tell you his name?"

"No. He knew my name though, but he never said his."

"Marla, would you tell me about him?"

"He had on a different coat, and he didn't have all those colors around him, but it was him."

Her response took me back twenty years back to Kentucky to that first Christmas without Mama.

CHAPTER ONE

Cedar Falls, Kentucky
1988

I DIDN'T THINK TOO much about redbirds until Mama and Daddy took me and my little brother on a Fourth of July picnic last summer. Daddy planned to go up to the mountain pass where the waterfall was because he knew it was one of Mama's favorite spots. From there she thought she could see Ohio and West Virginia and all the way up to the end of Appalachia. Daddy said she had some kind of special eyes if she could see all that, or else her geography was a little off, then he just laughed.

But Mama wasn't up to hiking the mountain trails that day, so we went out to Granny Grace's pond for our picnic and to go fishing. Daddy took my brother, Chesler, out in the boat. And that was when Mama—Diana Joy Harding—told me. Mama said it just like she woulda told me she was going to the store to get milk. "Katherine Joy, I'm going to heaven before long, not because I want to, but just because it's my time to go. I wish I could stay here to watch you grow up, but I don't think I'll be able to do that because I'm sick, and they've run out of ways to make me well."

1

Then I saw the tear roll down Mama's cheek. I wanted to hold her just like I used to hold my baby doll that cried real tears. In all my life I had seen Mama cry only one time because she was sad. That's when Grandpa died. The other times Mama just cried from laughing so hard.

I knew all about going to heaven because Daddy explained it to me when Grandpa went. Going to heaven meant Mama would be in a better place, but she'd still be gone. I wouldn't see her anymore 'til I got there. I couldn't brush her long red hair, or sing her made-up songs, or hear her stories about all the trouble she and Aunt Susannah Hope got in to when they were little girls.

Seeing Mama's tears made me cry too. So we just sat there on that quilt, and I held on to Mama like I was never letting her go to heaven without me. She was quiet for a few minutes before she said, "So, Katherine Joy, I want us to choose something that'll always remind you I love you and that I'm still there in your heart and in your memory. Something that will make you remember me every time you see it." It was right then that the redbird swooped down. A redbird. Just like Mama's hair. And that bird could sing like Mama too.

That was our last picnic. Mama got real sick, and she had to go to the hospital. Chesler and I stayed with Granny Grace for two whole weeks because Daddy was with Mama every minute at Cedar Falls Memorial. The doctors let Mama come home when she told them she had things to do. When Mama felt like it, she mostly played quiet games with us and cuddled with Daddy on the sofa to watch a movie. But when she didn't feel good and had to stay in bed, she made lists. I heard Daddy ask her one time what she was doing, and she said, "I'm making a list of the lists I need to make." Mama was like that.

She made lists of what we were supposed to do after she went to heaven. Her pink and yellow and blue slips of paper covered the bulletin board in the kitchen. The first thing on Daddy's list was to put up the bird feeders before winter set in. Learning to wash the dishes was at the top of my list, but there wasn't much on Chesler's list since he was only five.

Mama could even make dishwashing fun. She would go over to the cabinet by the refrigerator, and when she'd pull on the handle to open the drawer, it sounded like one of Granny Grace's squawking guineas. Mama would laugh and squawk back, and Daddy would get up and start toward the door. "I'll get my toolbox and fix that drawer right now." That was Daddy. He liked to fix things, but mostly he liked to make Mama smile.

Then Mama would say, "No, I like that sound. It's like the dinner bell, only when the drawer squeaks, it's time for Kate to wash the dishes." She'd take one of Granny Grace's homemade, checkered aprons out of that drawer and tie it around me. I stood right beside her to rinse the dishes after she washed them.

Mama would sing her bath time bubble song while washing the dishes. She'd put the bubbles from the dishwater on my nose and let me put bubbles in my hand and blow them against the kitchen window.

Mama had a song about everything. If she didn't know one, she'd just make one up. And when the redbird showed up in the cedar tree outside the kitchen window, Mama made up a redbird song. When I told her my teacher said the redbird was really a cardinal, Mama said, "It's a funny thing about birds. We call a black bird a blackbird, a blue bird a bluebird, but a redbird a cardinal. Kate, I can't think of one word that rhymes with cardinal, so if it's okay with you, let's just sing about the redbird."

When I mentioned to Mama that maybe we could get a dishwasher, she stopped washing, put down her dishrag, and pointed out the window. "Now, Kate, if there's nobody standing right here washing dishes, then that beautiful redbird in the cedar tree would have nobody to look at through the window."

Mama liked to walk down by the creek behind our house when she felt up to it. She said she hoped we would have an early fall because she wanted to see the red and gold leaves reflecting in the creek water just one more time. One afternoon after I got home from school, Mama put on her boots and the thick wool sweater Granny knitted for her, and we walked down the path to the creek and climbed up on the big rock at the bend. Really, it wasn't quite sweater weather, but it seemed Mama was always cold.

When we got to the top of the rock where Mama liked to sit, the sun was warm, and Mama just started singing the Irish folk songs Grandpa liked. And then right in the middle of one, she stopped and stared into the water and got real quiet like. I tried to hum to her, but then Mama started talking to me about life being like that stream. "Sometimes life's calm like that pool of deep water around the bend, and sometimes it's rough like the white-water upstream, but it's always headed somewhere, Kate," she said. "It's always headed somewhere.

But no matter how rough or calm the water, there are always the solid rocks underneath just getting smoother as the years go by."

Mama took my hand and held it with both of hers, but she didn't look at me like she usually did when she asked me a question. She was still looking at the water. "Kate, your life is going to get like the upstream white water for a while. You might not know which way you're going, and you might think you can't keep your head above the water, but you have smooth, solid stones underneath you, girl. You just remember that. Do you know what those stones are?"

When Mama talked like that, I felt the sadness squeezing me so much I couldn't breathe. I shook my head, but Mama wasn't looking at me.

"Katherine Joy, do you know what's going to keep your head up and keep you going somewhere?"

"You, Mama. You'll keep my head up." I was glad Mama wasn't looking at me so she wouldn't have to see my teary eyes. If she had seen me, I would have just told her it was that Kentucky breeze making my eyes water.

"No, Kate. I won't be here to hold your head up." Mama let go of my hand and pulled her sweater around her tighter. Then she pointed to the water's edge. "You think you can climb down there and pick up three smooth stones?"

"Yes, Mama. You want more than three? I can get 'em for you." I would have done anything to make Mama happy.

"Three will do it."

I scooted down from the top of the big rock to the edge of the creek, and I looked around until I found three smooth stones about the size of Granny's prize chicken eggs. I had to put two of them in my jeans pocket so I could climb back up to the top where Mama was sitting.

She took them from my hand. "Oh, good, you found three beauties. Now I want you to remember what I'm telling you, Kate. These are to remind you of the things that'll keep your head above water when I'm gone."

She handed me one of the rocks. "This rock is your faith. I taught you to pray when you were learning to talk. Praying is talking to God. Faith's depending on Him. You already know how to do that, and you just keep doing it, my sweet daughter, even when you don't feel like it, or you don't want to, or it doesn't make a dab of sense."

Then she handed me the second rock. "This rock is your family. You have your daddy and Granny Grace and Aunt Susannah and your little brother. They'll take good care of you, but you must remember life's going to get rough for them too, and you're one of their rocks. So sometimes, you'll have to be strong for them. You'll be the lady of the house when I go to heaven, so you'll have to help Chesler grow up, and you'll have to take care of your daddy and remind him of the things he might forget."

I wanted to scream, "I can't do that, Mama. I don't want to do it. You have to stay." But something stopped me before I said it out loud.

"And this final rock is for forever. Forever, Kate. Remember, life as we know it here on this planet is not all there is. There are things we cannot see here, but they are real. So you live and love knowing it's forever. Think *you can remember all that?" That's when Mama looked at me.*

I slowly repeated the words. "Faith, family, and forever. I won't forget, Mama."

She smiled and squeezed my hand. And that night after supper, she helped me paint the words on those rocks. Faith. Family. Forever.

Mama didn't make it to see the leaves change colors. She went to heaven in September not long after Chesler's birthday. She had been sleeping mostly for about two days. Granny was always on one side of the bed holding Mama's hand, and Daddy was on the other. They didn't talk much, but Daddy had Mama's favorite music playing, and the birds were singing outside.

It was in the middle of the night. Daddy came to my room and said it was time for me to say good-bye to Mama. He got Chesler up too. I went to their room and lay down beside Mama so I could feel her hair. Chesler didn't want to, so Granny held him in her lap. I tried to sing to Mama, but I couldn't. She woke up a little and whispered something. Granny must have understood because she held Chesler next to Mama's face. That was one time he was sweet. He kissed Mama on the cheek, and then he said the strangest thing. He said, "Good night, Mama. See you in the morning."

Mama smiled a little when Chesler said that, then she turned her head to me and said, "Give me your hand, Kate."

I found Mama's hand under the cover. It was warm and soft, and she squeezed my hand just a little bit. Then she whispered, "I'll always and forever love you, my sweet Katherine Joy."

"I'll always love you too, Mama."

Mama got quiet after that. Then she squeezed my hand a little bit more and whispered so soft, "Always remember what I taught you, Kate. Faith, family, and forever." Then Mama looked straight at Daddy sitting right behind me on the bed, and it was like her eyes just froze on him. Her hand wasn't holding mine anymore, but I was holding hers like I was the last thing to tie her to this earth.

Daddy sat there looking at Mama. He was sitting still like her too. Then he got up and took me by the shoulders. "Kate, I want you and Chesler to go with Granny now."

I didn't want to leave, but Granny said Daddy needed time alone with Mama. I turned around at the door. Daddy was kneeling on the floor, holding Mama and crying into her long, red hair.

———◆———

Everything changed that night Mama went to heaven and Daddy cried so hard. Sometimes it seemed like it was just last night, and sometimes it seemed like about a million years ago. But now it was almost Christmas, and I didn't know how to think about Christmas without Mama.

Daddy was at the table with Chesler while I washed the dishes again. I didn't mind though because I could think about Mama. The redbird was in the cedar tree. She sat there looking at me, doing what redbirds do, tweeting and pecking at the tree limb. She flapped her wings every now and then and shook the snow off the branches. I wondered if she wanted to be inside this warm house with me, my daddy, and my brother. If

Mama were here, she'd be singing the redbird song. I could almost hear Mama. "Be careful about rinsing out the sink so your daddy won't be looking at dried-up spaghetti sauce in the morning, and put away the dishrag like I taught you." Mama liked clean. The redbird flew away when I turned out the light over the sink.

I looked at Daddy sitting there with his long arm around Chesler, and I remembered how Mama used to look up at Daddy because he was so tall, and she talked about his broad shoulders and how he made her feel safe. Mama said Daddy was the handsomest man she ever saw with his brown eyes and high cheekbones.

I missed hearing Mama say things like that, and I knew Daddy did too. But he didn't have much time to be sad with all the things Mama left on his list, like helping Chesler do his reading assignments. Chesler could sing better than anybody except Mama, but he couldn't read too well yet. Daddy sat next to him listening to him read his rhyming words while he opened and stacked the mail.

Somebody sent Daddy a letter asking for money, and they sent address labels. Daddy handed the labels to me as he kind of mumbled, "Kate, maybe you would like these."

I sure did. They had redbirds on them. I figured Daddy didn't want them because Mama's name was on the labels too, and her address was in heaven now. I cut the pictures of the redbirds off the labels and stuck some on my pink notebook. I saved some for later.

When Chesler finished reading, Daddy said, "Let's make hot chocolate and play Skip-Bo. Nothing much to watch on TV tonight."

Daddy thought if he put chocolate milk in the microwave, it came out hot chocolate. I wished Mama had made a list about that. She heated milk, and melted chocolate and sugar on the stove, and put marshmallows on top. Mama knew how to do everything, and she made everything special, even a cup of hot chocolate. Daddy did things differently, but he was trying.

After Skip-Bo and hot chocolate Daddy helped Chesler with his bath and tucked him in bed. Then the bathroom was all mine. I got to stay up until nine thirty and read because I was going on eleven.

Right after Mama went to heaven, Daddy wasn't too good at doing bedtime. Some nights he would forget and not come to my room until after ten. I reminded him that Mama thought sleep was important for growing children. Daddy said, "If you can remember sleep's so important, why don't you remember to turn the light out at nine-thirty?"

Then I said exactly what Mama would have said if she were standing with her hands on her hips right here in this room. "John Chesler Harding, I don't think we're communicating."

When I said that, Daddy smiled a little. He hasn't missed too many nights since that conversation, and he was right on time tonight. He sat down on the bed, and I put my book away. "Kate, have you been practicing your lines for the Christmas pageant at church?"

"Yes, sir, two weeks left, and I already got them memorized." I didn't get a big part in the play this year. Pastor Simmons probably thought I might be too sad. But anyway, I knew my four lines, and I would be singing with the choir.

"What about your brother? You think he's ready too?"

"He can sing that solo backward, but he's gonna look funny in that sheep costume." Our choir teacher knew that would be a good part for Chesler. "Let's see, if Chesler's a little sheep and you're his daddy, that makes you...?"

"That makes me a ram."

"And Mama?"

"Well, then Mama would be an ewe."

That sounded weird, and I must have looked puzzled because then Daddy said, "Not you, y-o-u, but ewe, e-w-e."

I had to think about that a little. "Sure am glad he's not a little goat, then you'd just be an old goat." I was always trying to think of ways to make Daddy smile again.

He laughed a little bit. "Do you remember last year's Christmas pageant?"

"Sure, I remember." Last year when I was nine, I was the angel. Mama made me a whole costume, wings and halo too. I didn't know it then, but now I knew what gossamer was.

Granny Grace said to Mama, "That angel costume has to be of gossamer. Katherine Joy Harding will not wear a king-sized, white pillowcase with holes cut out for her head and arms. It must be gossamer."

Mama made a white dress with more layers than Aunt Susannah Hope's chocolate layer cake, and Daddy bent coat hangers to look like angel wings and a halo so Mama could cover it with gossamer. I didn't think there was anything Mama and Granny Grace couldn't do with a glue gun.

I got a rash two days before the pageant. Mama said, "Kate, I told you not to eat all those strawberries. Rash or no rash, you're putting on that angel costume, and you're going to recite the second chapter of Luke in front of the whole church." Mama was backstage with me at the pageant and just before it was time for me to say my part, she whispered in my ear, "Remember, Kate, angels never scratch."

Remembering all that made me and Daddy smile a little. "I wish Mama was here this year to hear my lines and to hear Chesler sing."

"I wish she was here too, Kate. I wish she was here all the time."

Before he said good night he told me he had to go in early for a meeting so Granny Grace would be here to get us ready for school. He kissed me on my head and went to the door. Then he did what he always did, turned around and said, "Little peep?"

And I said, "I know, no more peep from me." He turned out my light and closed the door.

It was quiet tonight, so quiet I thought I heard the snow falling. Some nights when it was quiet, I could hear Daddy down the hall, sitting in Mama's rocking chair in the sewing room. The floor creaked when he rocked, and I could hear him crying. He missed Mama so much, but I thought he cried too, because he was a paramedic, and he took care of people, but he couldn't make Mama better. He took care of Chesler when he got the fishhook caught in his leg and when he smashed his finger in the car door. Chesler kept Daddy busy with his accidents, but Daddy said cancer wasn't like having an accident.

Some nights I could hear Chesler crying, and I tried to get to his room before Daddy heard him because it made Daddy so sad. I would just lie down by Chesler, and we'd sing the songs Mama would sing quietly until he went to sleep. Mama had said I had to be their rock sometimes.

And some nights when I didn't hear Daddy or Chesler, I'd just put the pillow over my head so I couldn't hear my own self crying. I tried to remember what Mama said. Faith. Family. Forever. I missed Mama so much.

CHAPTER TWO

I WOKE UP THE next morning before my clock went off, and I was thinking about Christmas. We never had Christmas before without Mama. It wouldn't be the same. Nothing was the same. Like this morning, if Mama were here, she'd be waking me up just like she did every morning, opening all the curtains and diving into my bed beside me. Mama was gentle about most things, but not about getting up. She got up early every morning and thought the whole world should be up. Granny Grace told me it was because Mama was born at 5:00 a.m. and her clock was just set that way. I think Mama was born happy too. And if I didn't have a happy look when I woke up, she'd say, "Get that grumpy look off your face, Kate. You think life's gonna be better today because you're grumpy?"

She'd tickle me to make me laugh and say, "Time to get up and get going. God gave us another day to make somebody happy. That's our job—to make somebody happy today." Then we would lie quiet for a minute so I could think of one person I wanted to make happy that day. Every night before I said my prayers, Mama would ask, "Okay, Katie J, so who smiled today just because of you?" If I could tell her a name and what I did to make that person happy, then I could put the smiley face on my calendar. It was not easy to make somebody else happy every day when my happiness went to heaven with Mama, but I knew Mama would want me to try.

I was remembering early mornings with Mama when I heard Granny Grace coming up the stairs. She didn't look much like other grannies because she wore boots and blue jeans and her barn jacket most of the time, but she acted like one. She was a good cook, and she was kind most of the time. But she also knew how to boss people around like nobody's business.

I could get my own self ready for school, but Chesler needed help. Granny fed us and dropped us off at Cedar Falls Elementary School. We were about to get out of Granny's truck when she announced, "It's Friday, and you two are in for a big surprise tonight."

"The Blue Cow Cafe?" Chesler asked. We went to the Blue Cow Café up at the lake every Friday. It had a dock where we would sit in the summertime to watch the trout jump. Miss Bonnie, the owner, didn't even have to take our orders. When we sat down, she would yell to the cook, "Four Harding specials."

"No, going to the Blue Cow wouldn't be a surprise!" Granny laughed. "You'll see."

Waiting on that surprise made that Friday one of the longest days of my life. Daddy picked us up after school, and we went grocery shopping. When we got home, Daddy said Granny Grace and Aunt Susannah Hope and Uncle Don were on their let's-make-somebody-happy-today assignment. Aunt Susannah Hope was Mama's sister. She was red-headed and pretty like Mama, but she was serious about everything, not fun like Mama. Daddy always said Aunt Susannah Hope was skinnier than a knotty pine and her springs were wound too tight. Uncle Don was just what she needed. He was bald and chubby and laughed a lot, mostly at himself, and he didn't mind taking orders.

It was almost dark when they all showed up at our house with the big surprise: two boxes of pizza and a truck full of a Christmas tree and cedar branches. Uncle Don bought the tree down at the Christmas tree lot next to Smithson's Hardware store. Daddy and Uncle Don squeezed that tree through the front door, and Granny Grace was right behind them, sweeping up pine needles and telling them to hurry and get the tree inside before the pizza got cold.

After supper Aunt Susannah Hope said, "Kate, you and Chesler go get your favorite Christmas cassettes. We need to listen to some music while we decorate. And you big guys, get that Christmas tree vertical while I make the spiced cider." Aunt Susannah Hope knew Mama always made cider.

When the tree was standing at attention in the corner of the living room, Granny Grace started giving out orders like she did when she led the Fourth of July parade downtown. "John, you and Don get the Christmas decorations out of the attic. And Chesler, help Kate bring the small boxes into the living room."

Just when the smell of cider drifted into the living room, Granny Grace shouted an order to Aunt Susannah Hope. "Now don't you go scrimping on the cinnamon sticks." Granny knew how we liked our cider, and she knew my aunt. The music was playing, the cider was bubbling, and it looked like somebody dumped last year's Christmas in our living room.

The lights went on first, then the red and green balls, then we could open the special boxes. Chesler and I stayed out of the way while they were stringing lights, and when we had covered the bottom of the tree in balls, Daddy put Chesler on his shoulders so he could put some around the top of the tree.

Granny Grace tied cedar branches to the stair railing with red ribbon. She said to Daddy, "Now, John, I didn't get around to cutting any holly today because of the snow. Maybe you can take the kids for a walk down by the stream and cut fresh holly berries to go in the garland."

I knew Granny meant well, but I didn't really want to pick those berries. If we did, then the redbird would go deeper into the woods to find her food, and she wouldn't sit in the cedar tree while I washed the dishes. But I didn't say anything in front of Granny Grace. Her face turned red when someone didn't like her ideas.

When Granny finished with the garland, she started opening other boxes and taking stuff out, and Aunt Susannah Hope was right behind her trying to keep up. Only she wasn't opening. She was closing up the empty boxes and stacking them up at the bottom of the stairs. My aunt liked things neat. No clutter at her house. Daddy said it was because she didn't have children. Mama didn't mind clutter sometimes, but she did like clean.

I kept my eye on the three special boxes. The two red boxes were for the ornaments Mama made every Christmas, one box especially for me, and the other box for Chesler. My box had nine ornaments, and Chesler's only had four. I could hear Mama say, "One of these days you'll get married, and I'll give you this whole box of ornaments for your very first Christmas."

The third box, a gold one, held the ornaments we made for Mama. When I was three I made my first ornament in Sunday school—just a white paper cup with some glitter and stuff glued on the side, and turned upside down to look like a bell. It didn't really look like a bell, but Mama put it on the tree anyway and bought a special big box for it when Christmas was over. That bell made Mama smile so big I got to put two smiley faces on my calendar that night. And ever since I'd been making her ornaments for Christmas. Chesler started making ornaments last year, but I made him give Mama her ornament on a different day from me. That way Mama would be happy two times.

It didn't take long to empty those three boxes and put the ornaments on the tree. Daddy said, "It's time to put the angel on top, and Kate, it's your year to do that." He held me up so I could reach the top. That angel's halo brushed the ceiling.

Then Daddy said, "Chesler, hold your breath and plug in the lights."

Granny squealed when the tree lit up. "Would you look at that? Why, that tree is glittering like all the rubies and diamonds and emeralds in the window at Bishop's Jewelry."

We stood back to gaze at it, and I can tell you, that tree was really something. That morning, the pine didn't have any idea it was going to a dressing-up party. Somehow our lights and ornaments just made that old tree sparkle.

"Chesler, go get my small toolbox in the garage. It's time to hang the stockings." Daddy opened the box with the four Christmas stockings. Mama knitted one for each of us. When Daddy hung up only three stockings and closed the box with Mama's stocking in it, Granny Grace went to the kitchen.

She and Aunt Susannah Hope were getting out the Christmas mugs and the tray of Christmas cookies Granny made. Uncle Don sat down on the sofa to look at the tree, and Daddy disappeared like he did sometimes when Chesler asked him about Mama. He always came back.

This time he came back with two little red bags. There was some green paper sticking out of the top of the bags, but no ribbon. Then he called us to come to the tree. He said, "I don't know how to make Christmas ornaments like your Mama did, but I found some in a store I think you'll like. You can add them to your box after Christmas."

Chesler and I had to sit on the floor, back-to-back, to open the bags. Daddy watched. I took out the paper and pulled out a fancy box. Inside was a snow-white ball with a green ribbon on top and a redbird painted right on the side. I turned and saw Chesler had one just like it. I smiled. Daddy didn't know much about making ornaments, but he knew how to make us happy. We hung them side by side on the Christmas tree.

Granny Grace called from the kitchen, "Come on! We ate cold pizza, but we're drinking hot cider before we put out the manger scene."

I heard Aunt Susannah Hope tell Granny that she had cleared a place in the dining room for the manger scene.

"It'll be safe there so Chesler won't break it. You know how he's always running into things."

I shook my head at that. Sure, Chesler broke things, but he couldn't break the manger scene because it was made out of wood. Besides, Mama always put it beside the fireplace in the den so we could see it and play with it and tell the Christmas story over and over.

I might have gone to the woods and cut some holly berries even if I didn't want to so Granny's face wouldn't turn red, but this manger scene was not going in the dining room. So I yanked Chesler out of the kitchen while they were pouring cider. "Come on, Chesler, I need your help." We dragged the manger scene box out of the dining room, opened it, and dumped everything out on the floor, even Mary and Joseph and Baby Jesus and the leftover hay from last year.

I was getting all the pieces out, and Chesler was balancing one of the wise men on his head, when Aunt Susannah Hope walked in. She nearly lost her breath. I thought she might make a fuss, so I jumped in to explain. "Mama always put the manger scene here so we could play with it." I pointed to the hearth. If Aunt Susannah Hope made us move the manger to the dining room, I planned to start crying, then Chesler would whine, then Daddy would put a stop to all of it. But Aunt Susannah Hope seemed to lose all her words right then. She just stood there blinking hard.

Daddy and Uncle Don and Granny Grace came into the den to see what was going on. Granny patted my aunt on the back. "Breathe, Susannah Hope, just breathe." Granny handed her cup of cider to Daddy and got down on the floor with Chesler and me. She started her parade orders routine again, making sure that Mary and Joseph and Baby Jesus got to their places. "The holy family needs to come first," she said.

Chesler picked Joseph up. "He's not holey. I don't see any holes."

Uncle Don laughed. "Not that kind of holy, Chesler. Holy means dedicated to God, sacred."

Chesler nodded and put Joseph down by Baby Jesus. Then he picked up a wise man and started to put it behind Joseph.

Granny caught his hand. "Nope, not yet. The animals go next. Then the shepherds, because they were the first to get there. And after the shepherds you can put in the wise men."

Then Granny told us all about the shepherds and a dark night on a hillside. Granny asked, "What do you suppose the shepherds brought as a gift to the baby?"

We shrugged. Granny picked up the baby sheep. "Maybe they gave what they had. Maybe they gave the baby a lamb."

Chesler said, "No, they didn't give the baby a lamb because Mary already had one." Then he started singing, "Mary had a little lamb, little lamb, little lamb."

While Daddy and Uncle Don laughed at Chesler, Aunt Susannah Hope got that look on her face like she did when I picked up one of her china dolls. She told them they shouldn't be laughing and encouraging such behavior. I wanted to zip her mouth shut. My daddy needed to smile for once.

After we all quieted down, Granny told us about the gifts the wise men brought. We knew what gold was, and she explained about the frankincense and myrrh, how they were spices that smelled good and all. That made sense. A baby born in a barn needed something that smelled good.

Then Granny turned to us. "What are you going to give Baby Jesus for His birthday this year?"

Chesler picked up Baby Jesus from the manger scene. "But Granny, Jesus is in heaven, and He's got everything in the world. He doesn't need any more presents, and I don't know if He likes toys."

"Chesler, you're a smart boy, and you're right about Jesus being in heaven and having everything in the world. So He doesn't really need anything from us, but I don't think that's the point." Granny motioned for Chesler to come sit in her lap. "Come here, and let me tell you something important."

Chesler crawled across the floor into Granny's lap. "You know when you had your birthday party last summer?" Granny asked.

"Oh yeah, I remember, Granny. Mama made me a fire truck cake, and I got a dinosaur Transformer, and if I twisted his arm and his head around—"

I interrupted. "Yes, we all remember the robot, Chesler." I knew he would never stop talking about that robot, and I was more interested in what important thing Granny had to say about getting a present to heaven for Jesus's birthday. "So what's the point, Granny?"

Granny took Baby Jesus from Chesler and put it back in the manger scene. "The point is, you didn't need—I mean really need—the cake or the presents you got. But your mama needed to bake the cake to show you she loved you, and we needed to give you presents to cel-ebrate you, Chesler. Do you understand? Jesus doesn't need our gifts, but we need to give them. And when we give Him our best gift, no matter what it is, it makes Him so happy."

I knew Chesler didn't get it, and he was probably still thinking about that robot turning into a dinosaur, but I got it. I turned around and reached for the matches on the hearth. "Granny, can we light the Christ candle now, sort of like it's Jesus's birthday candle?"

Before Granny could answer, Aunt Susannah Hope said, "I don't think that's a good idea. It could set the straw on fire."

"Yes, ma'am." I didn't want to, but I put the matches down.

"Speaking of gifts, I found something for you kids, and I just can't wait till Christmas to give it to you." My aunt stepped into the kitchen and came back holding something that looked like a bucket covered in an old sheet. "I hope you like it. You can hang it near the kitchen window, and you don't even have to take it down after Christmas. Chesler, would you like to take the drape off?"

Chesler looked at Daddy to see if it was okay. Daddy nodded his head. Normally Chesler would have snatched that sheet off in a hurry, but he didn't. Maybe like me he had a funny feeling about what might be inside.

Chesler pulled the drape off slowly, dropped it on the floor, and stared at what he'd uncovered. Then he backed up, bumped into Daddy's leg, and buried his face in Daddy's khakis.

I stared too and clenched my fists. Why would Aunt Susannah Hope think we'd want a dead-looking stuffed redbird in a gold cage? I took the sheet and covered up the cage so we wouldn't have to see it anymore. Then I turned on my aunt.

"We don't want it." Aunt Susannah looked shocked and nobody said a word, so I turned to Daddy. "Take it, Daddy. Chesler and I don't want it. Please get it out of here."

Daddy grabbed me. "No, Kate. This is a gift. Your aunt thought you'd like the redbird, to remind you of your mama just like I thought you'd like the redbird painted on your Christmas ornament."

Chesler was still holding on to Daddy's leg. "But it looks real, and it looks dead."

"And it can't fly or sing, and it's in that stupid cage," I said.

Then Chesler started crying, and I couldn't stop shaking and started crying too. "Chesler's right. The bird in that cage is dead and cold and stiff."

Granny took my hand. "We hear you, Katherine Joy. Don, maybe it's best if you take that out of here for now."

But even when the cage was gone we kept crying, and Daddy didn't seem to know what to do or say. Finally he pointed straight up the stairs. "That's it. Both of you to your rooms right now. I'm not having this kind of behavior." His face meant business.

I ran up the stairs and dove into my bed. I didn't wait for Chesler. I just heard his door slam. I didn't care if he was crying or not, and I didn't care if Daddy was mad, and Aunt Susannah Hope was upset. I just wanted Mama. Why couldn't Aunt Susannah have died instead of Mama?

It wasn't long until I heard the front door close and Uncle Don's truck pulling out of the driveway. I lay still until I heard Granny talking loud to Daddy downstairs. She wasn't mad; she just talked loud 'cause she couldn't hear too good. I got up and went to my door to listen.

Granny said, "It's all right, John."

Daddy's voice was all choked up. "No, it's not. Nothing's all right anymore. I don't know how to do this without Diana. The kids, the work, the house. And Christmas. What is Christmas without her?"

They talking stopped 'cause Daddy was crying so hard. Just hearing him cry made me cry too. Then Daddy said, "I don't know what came over Kate tonight. I thought she was handling Diana's death so well."

Granny said, "Grief came over Kate. That's what came over her and you too. Just let her cry, John, and it's okay if you cry too."

"I do, but sometimes I'm afraid I'll upset Kate and Chesler."

"They need to see you grieve, John. Find yourself some time to cry, and let Kate do the same. She's trying to be your rock just like Diana Joy told her to, but she's still a little girl who's missing her mama."

I couldn't stand it anymore and just went back to my bed and put the pillow over my head. In a little while Daddy came into my room with Chesler. He sat down on the side of my bed and put Chesler in his lap. "Hey, little peep. You asleep?"

I moved the pillow from my head and sat up. "No, sir." Then I started crying all over again. "I don't want to be here, Daddy. I don't want to be anywhere if Mama's not there."

Daddy just grabbed me and rocked me and Chesler right there on the side of my bed. "I know, Kate. I know.

Sometimes I feel the same way. But I think if I weren't here, I'd be even sadder about what I'd miss. I'd miss you and Chesler, and decorating the Christmas tree, and so many other things. And look at all the things you'd miss if you weren't here." Daddy just kept rocking back and forth.

Then I thought about what Mama said about the rocks. "I'm sorry, Daddy. I'm so sorry." I moved over next to him, and we just sat huddled together like Granny's chickens did when a big storm's coming.

"No, Kate, I'm the one who's sorry. I'm sorry that I sent you to your room. I should have understood why you were so upset. And that bird in the cage? I don't blame you. It was creepy, but it's gone. We like redbirds that fly, and sing, and sit in the cedar tree, and peck on the window, don't we?"

"Yes, sir."

"Everything's okay now, and I'll try to do better."

"Me too, Daddy. I'll try to do better too." Chesler was sniveling.

"Hey, Ches," Daddy said, "you remember when Granny's dog, Grady, got hit by the car?"

"I remember," Chesler said.

I curled up closer to Daddy, wondering why he was talking about another sad day when we had enough sadness to last us forever.

"Do you remember how he was a sweet old dog, but when he got hurt, he growled at us and wouldn't let us get near him?"

Chesler perked up a bit. "Yeah, I was just trying to help him, but I thought he was going to bite me."

"Well, people are like that too, trying to protect ourselves when we hurt. When your Mama went to heaven, it was like we were all wounded, and sometimes we act like Grady. We get angry and snap at the folks who are just trying to help us."

"So that's why I snapped at Aunt Susannah Hope."

"That's right, and that's why I snapped at you too. We're just all hurting, missing your mama so much. But we still have each other."

We did a group hug, and Daddy kissed me good night. When he and Chesler left my room, Daddy started to turn out the light.

"Not yet, Daddy. I need to get ready for bed. I love you, and you too, Chesler."

"Love you too, little peep." Daddy closed the door.

I put on my gown, turned out the light, and crawled into bed. I turned my pillow over because it was wet. I lay there thinking about Grady and how he got sweet again when his leg got better. And then for some reason, I thought about what Granny said about giving Baby Jesus a birthday present.

That was when I got my idea.

Mama always said ideas were a lot like cars. "Most folks have them," she said, "but some of them you can't crank up and get out of the garage, and then others just fly." My idea had to fly. I just didn't know how to make it go.

CHAPTER THREE

I WAS GLAD TO go back to school. It was the only place that felt normal without Mama around. At school I could see my best friend, Emily, and go to art class, and I could even draw when Mrs. Maxwell wasn't looking. And sometimes I got to fill up the bird feeders.

Daddy put up bird feeders at the school and said it would be good for the children to watch the birds and take responsibility for filling the feeders, but I knew why he really did it. He brought a big sack of feed every week to school, and we took turns filling up the feeders every Monday morning. Just before Thanksgiving I saw the redbird for the first time at school, just sitting on that limb all by herself, waiting for the sparrows and chickadees to clear off the feeder. That's when I asked Mrs. Maxwell if I could move to a desk by the window. She let me. And since then I'd seen the redbird at the feeder almost every day.

Monday morning during math class, I was surprised when Laramie poked me with her pencil and pointed to the window. A redbird! My eyes stayed glued to that redbird perched on the feeder, ideas churning in my head.

Laramie poked me again. "You like cardinals, don't you?" she whispered. Everyone else was bent over their math sheets, scribbling away.

29

"How did you know?"

"Kind of obvious." Laramie pointed at my notebook covered in redbird stickers. "And you're always staring out the window at them when they're nearby."

"Yeah. So?"

Then she turned her head, and I could tell Mrs. Maxwell was looking at us. So we started doing long division again and acted like we'd been working on our worksheets the whole time.

"Kate?"

I was looking at that redbird and thinking, so I didn't hear Mrs. Maxwell the first time she called me.

"Katherine Joy? Are you drawing again when you're supposed to be listening? I don't want to have to call you the third time." If Mrs. Maxwell had used her playground voice, I would have heard her, but I wasn't sure she had one. She was so old I think it just wore out.

I looked up. "Yes, ma'am. I mean, no, ma'am, I'm not drawing."

"Put your notebook away, and come get your papers, please."

Mrs. Maxwell was still going through stacks of papers when I got to her desk. Eric was waiting too. He could annoy you just by looking at you. Mrs. Maxwell said his name more than anybody else's in class, even Laramie's.

"Look a here, Kate." He picked up the snow globe on her desk, turned it over, and watched the snow falling on a little manger scene.

Mrs. Maxwell said, "Eric, put that down. You know better."

I shook my head. Now why would a teacher put a snow globe on her desk and then not let anybody touch it? What good was a snow globe if you didn't turn it over to make it snow?

Mrs. Maxwell found the papers before it stopped snowing over the manger. She handed my papers to me and told me to put them in my take-home folder.

I said, "Yes, ma'am," and walked back to my desk. I put the papers away and got in line to go down the hall to the art room. Laramie was in front of me. I knew Emily didn't like her, but I wanted to talk to her. "Where'd you get the name Laramie, by the way? I always wondered. It's really pretty."

Laramie smiled just a little when I said that. She had been my classmate since second grade, but because I always played with Emily I hadn't gotten to know her very well.

"Oh, my mama and daddy were camping out in Laramie, Wyoming, when they thought it up."

"I guess you're lucky they weren't camping in Louisville."

She looked at me quick like she might be getting mad, but when she saw I was grinning, she smiled too. "Yep, real lucky."

"I can't wait to get to art class. Do you like art?"

Laramie turned around and smiled again. "It's my favorite class."

"Mine too, and I just love Miss Applegate."

"Yep, she's really nice, and she lets me do the kind of art I want to."

"What kind of art do you like to do?"

Laramie's face looked different, not like she was so mad like it did most of the time. "I really like to sew and make things out of fabric."

"Cool. My mama liked to sew too, but I don't know how. I just like to draw." We were almost at the door. "Have fun making whatever it is you're making."

"You too."

Miss Applegate was everybody's favorite teacher. She was young and pretty, like a cheerleader, and she said I had real artistic talent. She'd been teaching me to draw after school. Uncle Luke, Daddy's brother, liked her a lot. I saw them kissing last summer when we were all out at Granny's for a fish fry, and she came with Uncle Luke to Mama's funeral. I could call her Miss Lisa when she was with Uncle Luke, but I called her Miss Applegate at school.

When Daddy told Uncle Luke he should marry Miss Lisa before somebody else did, Uncle Luke said, "I need to finish medical school first. Then I'll think about it." I hoped he thought about it in a hurry. I'd like an Aunt Lisa.

When we got to art class, Miss Applegate already had the plastic containers with our names on them on the art table. I tugged at the lid to lift out what I made for my daddy. He liked anything to do with fishing, so I made him a bowl that looked like a fish. It could go on his dresser, and he could put his keys and change in it at night when he emptied his pockets. Miss Applegate showed me how to draw fish scales in the soft clay with a toothpick. And then she baked it so it would get hard and gave me some special paint to make the scales look shiny. She thought of everything, just like Mama.

After I finished Daddy's gift, I put it aside and lifted up a small wooden box. I had planned to decorate the box for Granny Grace, but her talking about a gift for Baby Jesus had given me a new idea. I needed that box for something special. What, I didn't know yet. But I would think of something.

First I painted it red. After I had carefully painted around the edges, I set the box on a piece of newspaper. When the paint was dry enough, I planned to put on some redbird stickers. After that Miss Applegate would spray it, and then it would be finished and ready for Christmas.

Eric sat across the table, painting a giraffe on a Christmas ornament. He pointed at the bowl I had made and mumbled, "I like that fish."

"Thank you. It's for my daddy."

He pointed at my red box with his dripping paintbrush. "Who gets that?"

I nearly snatched the paintbrush right out of his hand before it dripped on my box. "It's a special gift for somebody."

"For the teacher?" Eric dabbed some more spots on his giraffe.

"For my mama," I said.

"Your mama? You don't have a mama. Everybody knows she's dead."

Eric's words shoved me into a place where I didn't want to be. I didn't know whether to cry, or to run, or to just sock him in the nose. My mama had gone to heaven on September twenty-eighth, but no one had ever said out loud to me, "You don't have a mama. She's dead."

Laramie heard what Eric said and came and sat down beside me. "Don't listen to Eric. He's a dumb toad." Then she leaned over and whispered in my ear, "If you want me to, I'll take care of him after school. I'll make him sorry he ever said something like that."

I just bit my lip and shook my head. I believed Laramie could take care of him all right, but I didn't want her to get in trouble.

Laramie was as tall as Eric and the fastest runner in the class. She acted like a tomboy, but she didn't look like one, with her green eyes and long blonde hair. She often got in trouble for sassing or for saying ugly words, but she could be nice sometimes. She was the only one in the class who ever told me how sorry she was about Mama dying. I think it was because her mama was gone too. But I wasn't friends with her because my best friend Emily didn't like her. Emily was prissy and all into girly things, and Laramie? Well, Laramie was different and mostly stuck to herself.

I didn't talk to Eric or Laramie anymore. I just wanted to be quiet, put the redbird stickers on my box, and think about Mama. I finished, and Miss Applegate sealed the box and the lid with spray. When I wiped my face on the sleeve of my sweater and Eric started pointing at me, Miss Applegate told him the spray had made my eyes water.

CHAPTER FOUR

*T*HE LAST DAYS of school before Christmas break flew by, and finally it was Friday again. Daddy was working, and Aunt Susannah Hope had to take Chesler to the dentist, so Daddy asked Mrs. Peterson if I could come home with Emily after school. Mrs. Peterson and Mama used to be like me and Emily, best friends.

Everybody said Emily and I looked like sisters. Maybe it was 'cause we spent so much time together or maybe 'cause we were both skinny and had long, brownish hair the color of a dirty string mop.

The Petersons lived down Sycamore Drive only four blocks from Cedar Falls Elementary School and just a few doors down from Aunt Susannah Hope's. Mrs. Peterson said it was safe for us to walk home from school since there were two of us. Emily and I were both on the Honor Roll at school, and we didn't play with matches or knives, but we were not allowed to stay at home without an adult.

I'm not quite sure why it was safe to walk home in the snow, right past Glenn's busy filling station on the corner and the motorcycle repair shop, but it wasn't safe to stay at home by ourselves. I heard Granny say one time, "There are some seedy-looking characters at that motorcycle shop." She didn't know Laramie's dad worked there.

Laramie walked out the school door ahead of us. As soon as they spotted her, some of the older boys started in. "Hey, Laramie, want to race? Bet you can't catch us."

She didn't even look their way, she just said, "Shut your mouth, Jeremy, or you may catch my fist in your nose." They started whistling and teasing her about her long legs. So she stopped, and when she turned around what came out of her mouth would have gotten me grounded until I was eighteen.

We passed right by, but I felt bad for not speaking up or doing anything. "Those boys are so mean. Maybe we should invite her to walk with us."

Emily shook her head. "No way. Laramie's too trashy."

I felt sorry for Laramie. I heard Mama and Granny talking after Laramie's mama left in late August. They said Laramie and her daddy woke up one morning, and her mama was gone. Just plain gone. She had taken some of her clothes, a loaf of bread, a jar of peanut butter, and the car, and she never came back. Mama said, "It's just not right for a mother to leave her children like that. There's got to be more to this story."

Mama left me and Chesler, but not because she wanted to. I wasn't sure where heaven was, but wherever it was, I knew Mama was there and it was a good place. Laramie didn't know where in the world her mama was.

Laramie ran on ahead of us, and by the time Emily and I got to the motorcycle shop, Laramie was kicking a pile of beer cans around the parking lot. I raised my hand to wave to her, but when she saw us, she ran around the shop and disappeared.

"Don't wave at her, Kate, she's just trouble." Emily wouldn't even look in Laramie's direction.

Emily didn't know the difference between being trouble and having trouble. I wanted to tell her I would wave at Laramie if I wanted to, but that would just start a fuss. Emily always had to have her way. Anyway, I would just talk to Laramie when Emily wasn't around. Emily could still be my best friend and all, but somehow I thought Laramie was more like me.

Mrs. Peterson had the hot chocolate almost made when we got to her house. By the time we got out of our coats and mittens, she had put the marshmallows on top and started popping popcorn. She said, "You can eat it, or string it and hang it out back in the oak tree for the birds."

When we finished our snack, Emily wanted to see what I made in art class. Miss Applegate had helped me wrap up the presents with bubble wrap. So I unwrapped Daddy's fish first and laid it on the kitchen table.

Mrs. Peterson smiled. "Your daddy's just going to love that, Kate. You know how he loves fishing. What else do you have in there?"

Emily touched the bubble wrap. "Yeah, show us. We're good at keeping secrets."

So I decided to let them see the box.

"Oh, that's really pretty," Mrs. Peterson picked it up. "Who's it for? Your Granny Grace?"

I paused a minute, and then decided to tell them straight out. "I made this one for Mama."

Mrs. Peterson's face got a wrinkled-up look and she set the box down. "Oh, my goodness!" Adults said that when they didn't know what to say and thought something was weird. Emily just acted like she hadn't heard me. That was how she acted when Mama died too, like it didn't happen.

Then Mrs. Peterson got her perky smile back. "Would you like me to get the Christmas wrapping paper? You can do your wrapping here."

Emily said, "Yeah, Mom. Let's use my favorite paper."

I nodded. "Yes, ma'am, I would like to wrap the fish bowl."

Mrs. Peterson looked a little relieved that I didn't want to wrap Mama's box. She probably thought I changed my mind about giving my mama a present, but I hadn't. I had plans for that empty, painted box.

Mrs. Peterson brought in two rolls of Christmas paper, one of them silver with pink and purple Christmas balls, and the other gold with pine needles and pine cones. She put them on the table and looked at me. "Here, Kate, you get to decide which one your daddy would like."

I knew which one was Emily would choose, but I couldn't wrap Daddy's fish bowl in pink and purple. I took the one with pine cones. "Thanks, Mrs. Peterson. Emily's lucky to have you as a mom."

Mrs. Peterson smiled 'cause what I said made her a little bit happy, but somehow the smile didn't make it all the way to her eyes. They looked kind of sad and worried still. Anyway, I tried to make her happy. But lately, lots of people looked sad around me, as if I had a sign around my neck that said, "Be sad around Kate, her mama went to heaven." But at least I made her smile enough so I could put another smiley face on my calendar tonight.

After I finished wrapping Daddy's present, Emily and I went up to her room. Her room was pink like bubblegum. The walls, the carpet, the curtains, almost everything was pink. What wasn't solid pink was white polka-dotted. I didn't know how Emily lived in that cotton candy room. I liked my yellow sunshine room better.

Emily perched on her bed, and I flopped down beside her. "So," she said, not looking at me too close, "why did you make a present for your mama?"

"I always make a present for Mama at Christmas, don't you?"

"Yeah, I do. But my mom's here to get hers. Your mom isn't. So what's the use in making it?"

I moved away from Emily. "But Mama would want it. It would make her so happy."

Emily traced the polka dots on her bedspread with her fingers. "Okay, but how are you going to get it to her?"

"I don't have that part figured out yet. Putting it under the Christmas tree won't work."

Emily nodded. "Maybe you could leave it at your mama's grave in the cemetery and put a card with her name on it, sort of like the daisies you and your daddy take there."

"I already thought of that, but it won't work either, because Mama's not there, not really. Just because that's the last place I saw her doesn't mean that's where she is." I didn't like putting Mama in the ground because I knew Mama liked sunshine and flowers and warm weather. Daddy told me it wasn't really Mama there in the ground. He said Mama's body was like some old clothes she took off, sort of like butterflies leaving their cocoons behind. He said Mama, the real person she was and all that she felt and knew inside, now had on bright new clothes in heaven.

I didn't tell Emily all that. I just said, "There just has to be a way to get it to heaven. Maybe I could leave the box in the cedar tree outside the kitchen window and the redbird would take it to Mama."

Emily knew what Mama told me about the redbird. "No, I don't think that's a good idea. Some crow could just fly by and take it."

She was right. A lot of crows hung out in the woods by the stream this time of year.

Emily got quiet, and I thought she was trying to come up with a good idea, one that would crank up and fly. But then she asked, "Do you really think there's a heaven, Kate?"

Her question made me want to cry, but I just nodded. "I'm sure, really sure there's a heaven because Mama's there, just living in God's neighborhood."

"So where do you think God's neighborhood is?"

I shook my head. "I don't know, Emily. I think it's somewhere in the sky, higher that we can even see, and so far up it's not even blue anymore."

Emily didn't ask any more questions about heaven. She pointed at the box. "Why don't you mail it to Santa Claus at the North Pole and ask him to take it to her?"

Now Emily made straight As, but sometimes she could be just plain dumb. She probably thought the North Pole was closer to heaven. Who knew? Maybe it was. I didn't believe in the whole Santa thing anymore, but I didn't tell Emily that just like I didn't say anything to Chesler about it either.

I tried to be nice. "Santa has enough to do without worrying about my mama's present. I'll figure something out." I had an idea about who might have the answer, but I didn't share that with Emily.

The doorbell rang, and I was glad. I knew it would be Daddy. We'd stop at Aunt Susannah Hope's and get Chesler, and then take off to the Blue Cow for our Friday night supper. Grilled pork chops, succotash, hot biscuits, and cheese grits.

When we got to Aunt Susannah Hope's, Chesler met us at the door with his balloon and the bag Dr. Berg gave him. Like he would use a new toothbrush, and toothpaste, and dental floss. It was a wonder Chesler had any teeth left. He never brushed them the way Mama said to.

We got into the warm car and started singing the "Blue Cow Here We Come" song before we got to the corner. We'd been singing that song every Friday night since I could remember. Every time I heard it, I could taste cheese grits.

We drove up the street, passed the filling station, and right in front of the motorcycle shop, for no good reason I could see, Daddy slowed way down. He leaned over the steering wheel so he could see out the side window over my head.

I turned to see what Daddy was looking at.

Mr. Fields and Laramie were in the parking lot of the motorcycle shop. Her dad was pulling her arm, yelling something, and Laramie was standing her ground just like she did with those boys making fun of her after school. Mr. Fields yanked on her arm, and right then Daddy sounded the horn.

Mr. Fields's head came up. He looked in our direction, dropped his hand, and disappeared into the shop. Laramie took off running down the sidewalk, away from our car.

"What is wrong with that man?" Daddy muttered.

We rolled down the street, and Daddy kept looking in the rearview mirror, watching. I watched out the window till Laramie disappeared between two buildings.

"Do you know that little girl?" Daddy asked.

"Yes, sir. I know her a little. She's in my class."

"Do you think she'll be all right?" Daddy was still driving slow and looking in the mirror.

"I don't know, but I think so. She does a good job of taking care of herself." I remembered her offer to take care of Eric after school.

"Looks to me like she's had to learn to protect herself if that's the way her dad treats her."

"Her mama's gone." That's all I wanted to say.

"What do you mean gone?" Daddy looked at me.

"I don't know, just gone."

"What's her name?"

"Laramie. Laramie Fields."

"Oh, Fields, is it? Okay." Daddy stopped talking and nodded his head like he knew something I didn't know.

I didn't want to tell Daddy what I had heard Mama and Granny Grace say about Laramie's mama leaving in August. Granny Grace told me after Mama went to heaven that it was a sad thing children had to think about things like funerals and graveyards. Granny would probably add Laramie's mama to her list of things children ought not to have to think about.

We rode the rest of the way to the Blue Cow in silence, too sad to say anything. I knew Daddy didn't like what he saw, Mr. Fields yanking on Laramie's arm like that. Daddy always said hands were for taking care of people, not hurting them. And much as he wanted to, Daddy couldn't fix every hurt there was in the world. Mine included.

CHAPTER FIVE

*D*ADDY HAD TO work Sunday morning, so we went with Granny to church and then out to her farm for lunch. When we drove in, Grady met us all excited like, trying to wag his tail, but it was mostly sweeping the driveway. That old hound dog loved nothing more than chasing guinea fowl with Chesler. Grady didn't run too well since he got hit by a car, but he could almost keep up with Chesler. Granny and I stayed inside, looking through Christmas cookie recipes and keeping an eye on Chesler from the kitchen window.

Granny drove us back to town for pageant practice late Sunday afternoon. Almost as soon as we pulled out of the driveway, Granny said, "Chesler, let me hear you sing your song."

When Chesler sang, his mind just went off somewhere else. Not many people had heard him besides Daddy, Granny Grace, and me. But I knew that when he sang at the Christmas pageant, it would make people cry, and then everybody would go home talking about that little Harding boy sounding just like his mama. Granny Grace, Aunt Susannah Hope, and Chesler, they all sang like Mama, but I didn't. Guess God had to make some of us to listen.

Chesler practiced his solo all the way to Broad Street, his clear voice singing "All Is Well" even though we knew good and well it wasn't. How could it be when Mama wasn't here? It was like she was everywhere and nowhere all at the same time.

I thought about Laramie when we drove past the motorcycle shop. Pastor Simmons always said that whatever happened, God knew best, but something was not right about a daddy fighting with his daughter or children growing up without their mama.

Granny Grace dropped us off at the front door of the church. "I'm going over to your Aunt Susannah's, and I'll be back to pick you up when practice is over."

I hurried inside. I had to find Pastor Simmons to ask him something, but I didn't want Granny to know about it. I was glad she didn't stay at the church to watch us practice.

We were a little early. Chesler ran straight to the choir room and started practicing his solo with Miss Jan, so I wandered down the hallway to Pastor Simmons's office. Even though I could hear his voice talking to some ladies in the kitchen, it seemed kind of spooky to be in the church hallway alone, without any other kids.

I knew Pastor Simmons would walk by his office and see me, so I went in and sat down to wait for him. I sat up straight and tall in the chair in front of his desk, looking around at all the bookshelves. I thought there was just one Holy Bible, but Pastor Simmons had more Bibles than Aunt Susannah Hope had catalogs. I was glad. With all those Bibles he was sure to know the answer to my question.

I really liked the photos on the wall behind his desk, all picturing local scenes. One showed the springtime when wild flowers bloom in the woods and everything turns bright green. The summer photo showed the bridge down at the lake. Mama would have liked the autumn picture of the waterfall where we used to picnic, with its red and gold sycamores. But I liked the winter picture best: our old stone church with a blanket of snow around it and red ribbons tied to the lampposts.

"Kate, is that you? What a nice surprise." Just then Pastor Simmons came in smiling. He had blond, curly hair, and he wore little round glasses and a red sweater.

"Hello, Pastor Simmons." I really hoped he wouldn't think my question was dumb or something. But at least it would be easier to talk to a preacher wearing a red sweater.

He looked at me like Daddy checking out Chesler's skinned knees, but he didn't say a word until he sat down behind his big desk stacked with books and papers. "So, tell me, Kate, how are you this afternoon?"

"I'm just fine, sir." I pointed at the wall next to the window. "I really like your pictures. It's like a whole year in Cedar Falls."

He nodded. "Well, thank you. That's what my sister said when she took those pictures. My sister travels the world taking pictures, but her favorite place to take pictures is right here in the Appalachians. She says God took great pleasure in creating this part of Kentucky with its hills and forests and streams. And I agree with her."

"Mama always said Cedar Falls was closer to heaven than anywhere else."

He leaned back in his chair. "Well, just maybe your mama was right. So, tell me, Kate, what brings you to see me today?"

I told him I had some questions about my mama and about her dying.

"Well, we shouldn't talk about dying without first talking about living." He scratched his head. Then he asked, "Do you like to read?"

I nodded. "Yes, sir, I really like to read. I read all the time." I didn't tell him I read under the covers with a flashlight late at night. I didn't figure he needed to know that.

"Well, Kate, life's a lot like a book with a setting and characters and a few problems to solve." Then he asked me about my favorite book and if I remembered the characters and their problems.

"My favorite is *Charlotte's Web*, and how Charlotte saves Wilbur, and how Wilbur gets all sad when she dies."

He nodded. "That's a very good story. I'll have to read that to Harry." Harry was his five-year-old son.

Then he said in a soft, kind voice, "God is kind of like an author, Kate. He writes a story for each of us, and we are the characters in His story. Sometimes God lets us write a little bit of our own story, like choosing someone to be our friend. But God decides who our parents are."

I guessed that was what Mama meant when she said God picked me out to be her one and only daughter.

Then Pastor said, "We get to decide about some things, but God decides when the characters die and go to heaven to be with Him forever."

I remembered what Mama told me when we were sitting on that rock above the creek. Faith. Family. Forever.

What the pastor said sounded sort of like living happily ever after, but I wasn't so sure about that part. "I know Mama's in heaven, but I wonder if she's very happy without Daddy and Chesler and me."

"Oh, your mama's happy, Kate. She knows the end of the story. She knows one day you'll all be together again."

Talking to Pastor Simmons was better than giving book reports at school, but I didn't come to talk about books and stories and happy endings. I wanted to talk about dying and about Mama. But before I could say anything, Pastor Simmons said, "Life comes in stages, you know."

I knew about stages. For a while, Chesler threw a fit about eating vegetables. Granny Grace told Mama he was just going through a stage and not to worry about it. Sure enough, he got over it once he saw me eating my vegetables and getting dessert as a reward.

Pastor Simmons said, "I remember when you were born and you couldn't walk or talk. And when you could walk, you were a toddler, and being a baby ended."

I didn't remember being a baby or a toddler either.

Then he said, "You grew up more and went off to school. Your next stage will be when you're a teenager, and then you'll be a woman and get married and be a mother just like your mama." He went on and on about stages. Then he said, "The last stage is death, when we leave this world and go to be with God and all our loved ones who've gone before us."

I bit my lip hard. I didn't want to cry. I wanted to see Mama, but I was scared to die because I thought it hurt. Mama didn't seem to hurt; she just slipped away when she died. But with Daddy being an EMT, I knew about car wrecks and bad stuff like that.

So I asked Pastor Simmons, "Does it hurt to die?"

Pastor leaned back in his chair. "Well, Kate, did it hurt when you changed from being a baby to being a little girl?"

I shook my head. "I don't think so."

"Well, you're getting to be a big girl, and I'm going to be real honest with you." That's when he got up out from his desk and came around to my chair. He squatted down in front of me. I didn't think I was going to like his answer.

"Sometimes people die in accidents. Sometimes they're sick for a while like your mama, and sometimes they just get old and their bodies wear out like your grandpa's did. And sometimes people hurt before they die, but when they die, they're not sick or hurting anymore. And for your mama, because she chose to invite Jesus into her heart, dying was just like walking through a beautiful door into a perfect new place, a place where nobody has to say good-bye ever again. You don't like to say good-bye, do you?"

I nodded again. That didn't sound so bad. "But what if I grow up and I get old like Grandpa and just wear out? Mama won't know me when I get to heaven."

"Oh, Kate, your mama will know you. The Bible doesn't tell us all we want to know about heaven, but your mama would know you no matter what because the Bible says so. Would you like to pray now?"

What I really wanted was to talk to Mama, but I told him I had one more question.

He got up and rubbed his knees and leaned against the front of his desk.

"I made this special Christmas present for Mama, but I don't know where to put it so she'll get it in heaven. I was kinda hoping you could tell me."

He smiled. "Your mama has everything she wants in heaven. You don't need to give her a present. She knows how much you still love her."

"But my present would make her real happy. She could have it forever 'til I get there. There's just gotta be a way to get presents to heaven. Do you know what it is?"

He took off his glasses and rubbed his eyes. "Kate, I don't rightly recall anybody ever asking me that question before. Now I've read the Bible lots of times, and it doesn't say one thing about where to leave Christmas presents for delivery to heaven. I'll have to think about this one, and if you find out before I do, would you please let me know?" He was still rubbing his eyes when somebody knocked on the door.

It was Miss Jan. "Kate, time for practice."

Pastor said, "You come back to see me anytime, and I'm going to read *Charlotte's Web* again because you made it sound so interesting. I enjoyed our little talk."

We shook hands, and I left with Miss Jan. Chesler was singing "All Is Well" again while I climbed the steps of the choir risers. I wished singing alleluias made everything all right. If they did, I'd sing all the time.

I was thinking about when we would get home that night; it would be Chesler's turn to take the peppermint candy off the Advent calendar. Seven days 'til Christmas. Not nearly long enough to figure out where to leave Mama's Christmas present so she would get it.

Chapter Six

*J*UST LIKE SHE promised, Granny Grace was parked right outside the front door of the church when choir rehearsal was over. We headed back to the farm with her. When Daddy got off work, he would join us for supper.

Granny Grace and Grandpa lived in town when they were young. But when Grandpa sold his business and retired, he wanted to live out in the country and have a garden and chickens and goats and guineas. So they bought a farm and built a log cabin a few miles outside of town. Mama said that log house was like the one Grandpa grew up in out in the mountains. He never forgot home, and he never forgot being poor.

When my grandparents moved to the country, Aunt Susannah Hope was the first in line to inherit their old house in town. Since my aunt and uncle didn't have any children, they spent all their money and time fixing it up. They had piles of books to show them what an old house ought to look like. When they finished one room, they just went on to the next.

Meanwhile Mama and Daddy bought another house down the street and around the corner, next to the creek. Mama liked it because it was two-story, and she thought every kid should have a house with stairs.

Daddy liked it because he could stand on the back porch and almost cast his fly rod into the stream. One time I heard Mama tell him, "I don't want to live in a dollhouse or a museum like Susannah Hope. I want our house to be alive." I agreed.

After Grandpa died, Mama and Aunt Susannah Hope tried to talk Granny into moving back to town. Nothing doing. Granny Grace loved the farm, with its pond and trails and chickens, and so did I. "Grady keeps me company, and I don't think the town would enjoy Red Top crowing at four in the morning," Granny declared. And that was that.

Granny drove through town real slow on the way home from choir practice. "Just look at all those Christmas lights. They look even prettier in the snow." We passed a lit-up manger scene in front of the Methodist church, and Granny said, "Can you believe it? Next weekend, there'll be real live people and animals in that manger scene."

Chesler asked, "Will they have a real live camel too?"

"I seriously doubt we have any camels in these parts. They prefer sand, not snow."

Santa and his reindeer were blinking across the street in front of the bank. The way they blinked made Santa's sleigh look like it was flying, but Chesler's favorite was the giant snowman in front of the tire store. Every time Chesler saw it, he sang "Frosty, the Snowman."

When we drove by the motorcycle place, Granny said, "Kate, your daddy's been talking to me, and we were thinking about inviting the little Fields girl over to spend some time with you during the holidays.

Somebody ought to be nice to that little girl, especially at Christmas."

I guessed that was Granny's way of saying we were going to be the somebody. Last summer Granny and I went down by her pond to pick blueberries for a pie. She said her neighbor was sick and a pie would make her feel better. Every week Granny took baskets of food to the poor families who lived in the hollers over by the river.

As we picked blueberries, I asked, "Granny, why are you kind to everybody?"

"Why, child, I'm building my mansion in heaven, and with every act of kindness, I'm adding another brick."

Granny's mansion is gonna be big and tall.

The bucket was nearly full of blueberries, and Granny was sweating and breathing hard. "Let's rest a minute before we walk back to the farmhouse." So she just sat right down on a log and motioned for me to sit next to her.

Then Granny started talking, and I never forgot what she said. "Katherine Joy, what's wrong with this world is that folks live like this old earth is home. But it's not. Living on this planet is like going camping. You pitch your tent, and you go berry picking or fishing or walking around in the woods or playing a game with your family. You don't spend all your time trying to make the tent more beautiful or more comfortable, because it's not home. Just a waste of your time, and you'd miss out on lots of things that would make you and somebody else feel real good. Remember, you're just gonna spend a few nights in that old tent, then you'll be going home."

Then she wiggled a bit on that old log and looked straight at me. "Katherine Joy," she said, "You live at 804 Creek Meadow, but that's not your permanent address.

That's just your tent, and you'll probably have a few more tents in your lifetime. But you remember, a couple of years ago you made a choice to live your life God's way and accept what Christ did for you on the cross. That means your permanent address is in heaven, so don't you be wasting time. You be like your mama, good and kind, always helping folks who hardly even have a tent. Then one of these days, you're going to have the most beautiful mansion you can imagine to live in forever, and I'm going to be your next-door neighbor." Granny laughed then and got up off that old rotten log, and we walked all the way home holding hands.

I didn't understand it so much then, but I did when Mama died. Granny Grace knew Mama was going to heaven soon, and she was thinking about what Mama's mansion might be like.

I was glad Granny Grace told me all that last summer. I didn't want to waste any time. I wanted to gather some bricks for my mansion in heaven. I wanted to be Laramie's Somebody, so I patted Granny on the back while she was driving and said, "Yes, ma'am. We can invite Laramie over anytime you want to."

Granny Grace slowed down at the red light, and when she saw no one was coming, she just kept driving toward the farm.

Chesler stopped singing. "Granny Grace, is it okay now to run red lights?"

"No, it is not, but I need to get home in a hurry. Something's in the oven, and if the deputy stops me, I'll just invite him home with me for charred chicken pot pie." Granny hardly slowed down when she turned off the dirt road onto the lane going down to her place. We rounded the curve to the carport leading out back on two wheels.

Grady met us before we could open the doors to the truck, and the smell of chicken pot pie met us at the back door. Pot pie was one of Daddy's favorites, so Granny was going to make him smile tonight. Granny Grace laid her keys on the counter and put on her red Christmas apron and told us we could go look under her Christmas tree to see if there were any presents with our names on them. Chesler took off so fast he probably left skids marks on the oak floor trying to get to the tree first. When I walked into the room, I looked at the tree and stopped.

Chesler headed for the boxes and started pushing them, looking for his own name.

I grabbed his shoulder. "Quit what you're doing and look. Look at the top of the tree."

He crawled out backward from under the tree and rose up on his knees. His eyes got as big as saucers. "Is that the redbird Aunt Susannah gave us?"

"Uh-huh."

Granny had put Aunt Susannah Hope's redbird on top of her tree. But somehow, seeing that bird on the top of a Christmas tree didn't bother me near as much as seeing it in a cage. And if it did, I wasn't about to say a word about it.

Chesler didn't say anything either. He just shrugged and went back to digging through the presents. I was right. Daddy smiled big when he smelled the chicken and saw the steam rising out of Granny Grace's pot pie in the middle of the table. "A perfect ending to a perfect day." That meant he'd had a quiet day at the station, with no injuries, accidents, or anybody real sick. Daddy liked quiet days. Mama used to ask him how his day was. "Fine, good, or perfect" meant nothing happened. But when he said, "Let's talk about that later," I knew it meant something not good. Daddy didn't like to talk about bad things in front of me and Chesler.

After we ate, Daddy asked Granny if she had two pieces of paper and two pens. "It's time Chesler and Kate wrote their letters to Santa. Got to mail them in the morning if they're going to reach the North Pole in time. Christmas is coming up fast."

Granny Grace brought the paper and pens to the table, and she sat down next to Chesler. He couldn't write so fine, and Daddy said the writing had to be good so Santa Claus could read it. Chesler may not write very well, but he didn't have any trouble telling Granny what to put on that list. New skates, a reel and rod, a cassette tape player for his room, and a sled. He just kept going, and Granny finally told him to slow down because Santa wouldn't have room in his sleigh for any other children's gifts.

I didn't believe in Santa. I knew Granny Grace bought us the presents under her tree and the ones at our house would come from Daddy. But to play along, I took my pen and in my very best handwriting, I thanked Santa for all the art stuff he brought me last Christmas, the easel and drawing pencils and paint stuff and a sketch pad. And if Daddy was Santa, maybe my note would make him smile. Then I sat there a long time thinking, and finally I put only one thing on my list. Chesler was still telling Granny what to put down and what to erase, and Daddy just sat there quiet like, but I knew he was looking at my paper. He saw the word camera and my name at the bottom.

"What kind of camera do you want?"

"It doesn't really matter, just one that takes pictures." I liked to draw, but I couldn't draw much yet from just thinking about it or trying to see it in my head. But I knew if I had a camera, I could take pictures of things I wanted to draw, things like the redbird sitting in the cedar tree, or the daisies growing in the backyard, or maybe even a person.

"Santa ought to be able to find the best camera. Is there anything else you want to put on the list?"

I knew what I wanted most of all, but putting it down on a list for Santa Claus wouldn't do any good. I just wanted Mama back. I wanted it more than anything.

When I was real young, I told Grandpa one time before he went to heaven that I wanted some ice cream. When he said he didn't have any, I started crying and fussing. But he just said, "I don't have any ice cream, Kate, and I'm sorry you're not old enough yet for your wants not to hurt you."

Grandpa was smart, but what he said didn't make sense. What I wanted—Mama to come back—hurt a lot. And Daddy wanted the same thing, and his want made him sad. How old did you have to be not to hurt when you didn't get what you wanted? Granny Grace was old, real old, but not getting what she wanted still hurt her. That was why she put that redbird on top of her tree.

Me and Chesler folded our letters and put them in an envelope. Daddy said he would address and mail the letters first thing in the morning. "Okay, go get your things together. We need to hit the road."

We went to get our things, and I finished before Chesler. Daddy was helping Granny clear the table when I got back to the kitchen door. They didn't know I was listening.

"I blew the car horn, and if Kate and Chesler hadn't been with me, I think I would have stopped and had a talk with that guy. Nobody yanks on a little girl like that."

"I can't imagine what that child's living in, her mother gone and her daddy treating her like that. Did you ever hear any more about her mother?"

"All I know is that no one's seen her since she left in August. Rumor has it that she went back to her family in upstate New York. Nobody around here seems to know much about the Fields."

"That's got to be hard on a little girl. She really needs a friend. I've already talked to Kate about her, and she's agreed to invite her over sometime during Christmas break."

"You're a good woman, Grace, and I don't know what we'd do without you."

"I don't say it enough, John, but I want you to know you're doing a great job with the kids. What you're doing is not easy."

"No, it's not. It's the hardest thing I've ever done. I just never dreamed I'd be without Diana. Sometimes I reach for her in the middle of the night, or I think I hear her voice and turn to see. I look at the kids, and I still can't believe she's gone, and they're growing up without her. Kate's having to grow up fast without her mama, Grace."

"I know, I know. She works hard at taking on responsibilities that aren't really hers, but you have to let her, you know, and you have to let her be a little girl sometimes too."

"That's the hardest part, knowing when. She's like a mother hen to Chesler most of the time, and then I look in on her sleeping some nights, and she looks like my little baby girl. I'm not sure she's buying all this Santa stuff this year. I think her mama dying just took some of the magic out of her little-girl life."

"You're probably right about that, John." Granny chuckled. "Diana made our lives more fun, didn't she?"

"Yes, she did. Man, I really miss her. I knew how sick she was for a year, and I still wasn't prepared for her dying. My life'll never be the same."

"Your life will be different, but it will be good again, John. You hold on to that. It will be good again."

I walked into the room. Granny was washing dishes, and Daddy was putting the milk in the refrigerator. "Got everything, little peep?"

"Yes, sir. Chesler's coming."

"Good. Granny tells me you're inviting the little Fields girl over to play next week. I think that'll be a good thing to do."

"Granny said we could come out here to play."

"She did, did she? Well, if she's having chicken pot pie for lunch, then I'm coming to play too." He patted Granny's shoulder.

Chesler dragged his bag into the kitchen, and Granny dried her hands on her Christmas apron and followed us to the back door. She kissed Chesler, and she hugged Daddy and me. Granny's got comfortable arms, like my favorite pillow. "Okay, you call Laramie and ask her if she can come on Tuesday." Then I saw her wink at Daddy.

CHAPTER SEVEN

*A*LL THE WAY home Chesler talked about his Christmas list. "Man, when I get my new skates, I can cut figure eights on Granny Grace's pond just like you, Daddy. But what if Santa thinks I shouldn't have the train track and the rod and reel? I don't know how he's going to pick which one to bring." Chesler was so wound up I wondered when he was going to stop to breathe. "I like them both, but if he can only bring one, let me think. I hope it's the rod and reel, then when the pond thaws out, we can go fishing with my new fishing rod. And…" He sat in the backseat yapping like he thought someone was listening to him. When he quit talking, he started singing Christmas songs.

It had snowed most of the day, but finally it was slowing a bit. The streets were quiet, because most folks were home on Sunday night at nine o'clock. We had been gone all day, Daddy at work, and me and Chesler at church with Granny, so I knew the house would be cold.

When Daddy turned onto Creek Meadow, he said, "Nothing warms up a cold house like a fire. Let's build us one, roast some marshmallows, and watch a movie."

"But, Daddy, it's bedtime," I reminded him.

"Hey, did you forget? You're out for the holidays, and I don't have to go in so early tomorrow. Maybe we could just forget about bedtime tonight and sleep in tomorrow morning and have waffles for breakfast."

That meant cold waffles...or cold eggs. Daddy hadn't figured out how to cook yet so we never got both of them hot at the same time.

Daddy pulled up the driveway and pressed the button for our garage door. "I'm making chili tomorrow night because Uncle Luke's coming home from medical school for the holidays, and he loves chili." Daddy was always happy when his brother was around. Uncle Luke was the only close family Daddy had left, since his parents died before I was born and his aunts and uncles had moved away from the area. Two whole weeks with Uncle Luke. Maybe Miss Applegate would be coming over a lot. She could help me with my drawing.

We climbed out of the car, and Daddy let us in through the kitchen. "Go put on your pajamas, and I'll get the fire started. Then we'll have a family meeting and vote on what movie to watch."

That meant it'd be a Western tonight. Daddy said we would take a vote, but he took turns voting with Chesler and then with me. So it wasn't really voting. It was Chesler's turn tonight. Most of the time I picked something Daddy and Chesler liked to watch anyway. Getting them to watch a movie kept them busy so I had time to think or draw.

We were running up the stairs when Daddy hollered, "Hey, you want popcorn or marshmallows?"

I yelled, "Popcorn!" I grabbed Chesler's arm and gave him the eye.

Chesler yelled, "Marshmallows!"

That way we got both. When we got to the top of the stairs, we made our thumbs-up sign, curling our fingers and shaking hands and doing a thumbs-up and touching thumbs. Uncle Luke taught us that sign. He said that he and Daddy learned to do it when they were boys as a sign they were brothers and they stuck together.

Chesler could be annoying, but as his big sister I had to look out for him. That was on one of the lists Mama made for me. One list was about helping Daddy because Daddy wasn't so good at remembering things, like taking out the trash before it smelled, and making the grocery list before we went shopping, and remembering everybody's birthdays. Another list was about helping Chesler. I was five years older than Chesler, so I already knew things he didn't know yet. Mama wanted me to help him learn to read, and to make sure he brushed his teeth and his hair, and to remind him about being kind so he could put smiley faces on his calendar.

And Mama wanted me to wake Chesler up and start the day happy. That was the hardest thing on my list.

As I put on my fuzzy slippers, I heard Chesler running down the stairs, and I could already smell popcorn. I headed for the den. I was right about the movie. Cowboys and Indians again. Chesler was the only kid I knew who didn't like movies with cartoon characters. We grabbed the blankets Granny made for each of us and wrapped up. Then we sat lined up on the sofa like blackbirds on a fence and passed the popcorn basket back and forth 'til it was all gone. When Daddy reached for the bag of marshmallows, I told him I was sleepy and wanted to go to bed. He said okay but not to get up too early. I took my blanket and started up the stairs.

I wasn't really sleepy, but I was tired of horses and shotguns and men spitting in the campfire, and I wanted to work on my gifts for Granny Grace and Aunt Susannah Hope. Daddy wasn't big on shopping, and Mama always said a homemade gift was the best kind anyway.

Before I got to the top of the stairs, I stopped. "Daddy, make sure Chesler brushes his teeth before he goes to bed. You know what Mama said about sticky marshmallows hugging teeth. They need a good brushing."

"Yes, Kate, I'll make sure of it."

I had done what Mama put on my list, so I headed to my room. I turned the covers back on my bed and pulled my sketchbook out of my desk drawer. The second I heard the television go off, I planned to close my sketchbook, turn out my desk light, and jump into bed just like I'd been there all the time. Even if my light was out, Daddy would still come in to check on me.

Before I started drawing, I got my page of stickers out of the drawer. They were just little yellow round stickers about the size of a nickel. I asked Mama one time why we couldn't just buy some smiley-face stickers. She drew two dots and a half a circle on one of those yellow dots and said, "Why, if we bought smiley faces then we wouldn't get to make our own! And that's half the fun!" So I put big dots with glasses on them to look like Pastor Simmons, and I peeled it off the paper and stuck it on my calendar for today. I had made Pastor smile this afternoon when I talked to him about my favorite book.

I could have put two stickers on December 18 because I made Granny smile when I told her I'd invite Laramie over to play. Putting that smiley face on the calendar before I went to sleep was as important to Mama as brushing my teeth or saying my prayers. We always talked about the kindnesses we'd seen or done that day, and then we said our good-night prayers.

The wind was blowing, and it kept knocking that elm limb against the window. I pulled out my sketchbook. Without Mama, I didn't know how to make much, but I could draw. I had the idea to draw a picture of Mama as a Christmas present for Granny Grace and Aunt Susannah Hope. So on Saturday I had gone through all ten Books of My Life. That's what Mama called the picture albums she made for Chesler and me. She made one every year and said it told all about our lives in pictures. My birthday was in April, and it looked like if I wanted a Book Eleven, I'd have to make it myself. But there wasn't much I wanted to remember about this year except Mama being alive.

I had looked at all the pictures with Mama in them for a long time. I took the ones I wanted out of the book, but I was careful to label them because I wanted to put them right back where Mama had them.

I opened up my sketchbook and picked up the photos I had chosen. I looked at them a long time, and then I chose one and began to draw. I made lots of lines, and sometimes my hand accidentally smeared them so the picture got all smudged and blurry, kind of the way I saw Mama in my mind now. I didn't want to forget how Mama looked. My pencil could put the lines back on the paper, but nothing could make me remember Mama any better. I just had to close my eyes and try real hard to see her. And I'd draw her over and over again so I wouldn't forget.

I was making the long strokes of Mama's curly hair when I noticed the silence. I looked at the clock. Ten after eleven and the movie had ended. I crammed my pencils in the cup and shuffled the pictures together and closed the sketchbook. After I turned out the light, I jumped into bed, blanket, housecoat, slippers, and all. I lay quiet, pretending to be asleep. Soon I heard Daddy's footsteps coming up the stairs, slower than usual. Chesler had done it again, fallen asleep, even after eating marshmallows. Daddy knew better than to wake him up, so he was carrying him up the stairs. That meant no teeth-brushing. Sometimes I thought Chesler's goal for the day was to get out of brushing his teeth.

It wasn't long before my door opened and Daddy came in. He bent over the bed, brushed my hair off my cheek, and kissed me. "Good night, little peep," he whispered like he always did. Then the door closed behind him, and he went to his room. I just kept my eyes closed, and I was looking in my mind, remembering Mama's face, when I went to sleep.

Sometime later I heard the phone ring. Nobody in the Harding house liked it when the phone rang late at night. Then I heard Daddy talking. I couldn't understand what he was saying, but before long before lights came on and doors opened and closed.

Daddy came into my room first. He sat on the side of the bed and put his hand on my cheek. When I opened my eyes, Daddy said, "Little peep, you have to get up. I have to go to work."

I knew that meant something bad had happened. "Don't worry about getting dressed or taking anything with you, but just hurry. You can go to back to bed when we get to Aunt Susannah Hope's." Then he went to wake Chesler.

"Don't wake Chesler up, Daddy. You know how he is." I looked at the clock. It was a little after two. I still had on my slippers and housecoat so I just went downstairs wrapped in my blanket. I got Chesler's blanket off the sofa and met Daddy at the door to the garage. I knew he wouldn't think to wrap Chesler up, and I knew better than to ask Daddy what was going on. He didn't like to talk about bad stuff.

When we got down the street to my aunt's house, the front porch light was already on, and I could see her and Uncle Don through the glass door, standing there waiting on us. But before we got out of the car, Daddy said, "Katherine Joy, you're a big girl now, and I want you to pray before you go back to sleep. Pray that it'll stop snowing." He squeezed my hand and said, "I'll pick you up in the morning."

CHAPTER EIGHT

*U*NCLE DON TOOK Chesler out of Daddy's arms and carried him to the guest room down the hall. I followed Uncle Don. "I'll just sleep in the room with Chesler in case he wakes up in the middle of the night and doesn't know where he is."

"You're a good sister for thinking about that, Kate." Aunt Susannah Hope tucked us in and turned on the night-light before she said good night and closed the door.

Even though I worried about Daddy, and the wind howled outside the windows, I felt sleepy. But if Daddy asked me to pray about something, I figured it must be important. "Dear God, if You would, please just hold the clouds in Your big arms so the snow won't come down for a while. Somebody must be in trouble, and snowing might make it worse. And dear God, please keep Daddy safe while he's out trying to help somebody. My mama's already in heaven, so please don't let Daddy get hurt or lost in the snow. Amen." I made sure Chesler was covered up, and I rolled over.

When I woke up, I smelled bacon, and I could hear Daddy's voice in the kitchen. Everything must be all right. I got out of bed and looked out the window. The sky was gray, but no more snow, and Daddy was safe.

"Thank You, God, for listening to me and answering like I wanted You to this time."

I was heading down the hall to the kitchen when I heard Daddy. "Nobody's seen her since nine o'clock last night."

Somebody had gone missing. I stood in the hallway outside the kitchen and listened. "We've got to find her soon or it could be too late if she's injured or not prepared for this icy weather. This is about the worst December on record. All I can think about is what if it were Kate or Chesler out there in the cold. I want to see the kids, and then I have to go back out."

I didn't want Daddy to go back out. He was just here to check on us and have a warm breakfast. I knew it. Then, he'd go back to help find whoever was gone missing.

"Don't wake the children; they're still asleep. Do the police think somebody took her?" Aunt Susannah cracked eggs while she talked.

"I guess it's possible, but I don't think so. There was no sign of forced entry, and her coat, hat, boots, and mittens are missing. Looks like she left walking, but the snow filled in her tracks so we couldn't follow them."

I could hear Aunt Susannah from across the kitchen. "At least it stopped snowing. Surely you'll find her. How did they find out she'd gone missing?"

Then Daddy said, "The police said Fields had some of his buddies over to watch a game last night, and things got rowdy. The Harrisons next door heard the ruckus, and Roger walked over at about midnight. He didn't like what he saw going on through the window and decided to call the police. When the police got there, they found some drug paraphernalia. Fields swore it wasn't his, but they arrested him for possession and threatened to take him to jail. He told them he couldn't go, he had a daughter asleep in her bedroom. So they checked, but no Laramie."

Laramie? Something had happened to her. Missing. Maybe lost. I wondered if she just packed her bags like her mama did and left, or maybe she was trying to find her mama. Either way she was gone. And nobody knew where she was.

When I stepped into the kitchen, Uncle Don and my daddy were sitting at the breakfast table, Daddy holding his coffee cup in both hands like it was the only thing in the world keeping him warm. He looked up when I stepped into the room, and I hugged him hard before he could put his coffee cup down. Then I sat in the chair next to him.

"Good morning, little peep. Did you just hear what I said? "

"Just a little bit."

"Well, you've done a lot of growing up this year, and you need to know what's going on. It looks like Laramie has run away from home. Do you have any idea where she may have gone?"

I shook my head. "No, sir."

"Has she ever talked about a place she likes, a person she visits, or anything like that?"

I drooped a little. "No, we don't talk much." Maybe if I'd been a better friend to Laramie, made her smile some more, she would have come to me instead of running off into the cold and snow.

Daddy had that pinched little frown line between his eyes that he got when he thought on something too much, and he didn't say anything more. I knew he was worried. He was probably remembering Friday afternoon when he stopped in front of the motorcycle shop and saw Laramie's dad yanking her arm.

Aunt Susannah Hope put breakfast on the table for Daddy and Uncle Don. "Don't worry, John, I'll take Kate and Chesler home to get dressed and to get whatever they want to play with today. They can spend the day with me."

Daddy asked, "Don, what are you doing today? Think you could help in the search? The more folks we have looking, the better our chances are of finding her."

"Sure, let me make a couple of calls." Uncle Don ran his own accounting business, so he set his own hours.

"Thanks, Don. And Susannah, tell Chesler I'm sorry about missing breakfast with him and I'll be back as soon as I can." Daddy gave me an extra-long hug and told me to keep praying.

After Daddy left, Aunt Susannah Hope sent me to wake Chesler up. I sat down on his side of the bed and shook his arm. He opened his eyes and looked around, shaking his shaggy head of hair. "Why are we at Aunt Susannah's?"

I told him Daddy had been called out to work. "Come on, Chesler, get up. Aunt Susannah Hope's taking us home to get dressed and to get some things to play with because we're spending the day with her." I didn't tell him about Laramie because I didn't think he needed to know.

We went to the house to get dressed before breakfast. Aunt Susannah Hope liked to do things in order. The house was cold, so I dressed in a hurry. I got to thinking about Laramie, wondering if she was warm or where she might be.

I could hear Aunt Susannah Hope asking Chesler what he wanted to wear. That boy had a mind of his own when it came to picking out clothes. Mama always picked out two outfits and let him choose one. That way he didn't come out dressed like Eric on costume day at school.

Mama had told me one time that Aunt Susannah Hope and Uncle Don couldn't have kids. I thought that might be why she didn't smile much. And she didn't know how to handle us very well. She wanted to be a good aunt, I could tell she really wanted to, but she just didn't know how.

I knew she would need help with Chesler, so I marched into his room. "Chesler Mackenzie Harding, listen to me. We're leaving in exactly three minutes. If you want to spend all three minutes deciding on which sweater to wear, that's fine. That just means you won't have time to get your games or movies to take to Aunt Susannah Hope's."

Chesler dressed in a hurry and got his toys, and we went back to my aunt's house. She hovered until almost lunchtime, making us play board game after board game. I thought I'd get a break when she started to fix lunch, but she said it was best if we came with her to the kitchen.

"I'm going to stay here on the sofa and read." I really needed some time to myself.

"You can read after lunch. Besides, I have a surprise for you in the kitchen."

Chesler jumped up and skidded into the kitchen ahead of her. Dragging my feet, I followed behind.

Her kitchen was like a page out of a magazine. Her whole house looked like a dollhouse. Too much white furniture and lace for me, and everywhere I looked was a bowl of dried flower petals that smelled funny. Why would she want pale, dried-up flowers when she could have fresh ones? Aunt Susannah pointed to the kitchen table, where she had set out two coloring books and two boxes of crayons. "I was planning to put these in your Christmas stockings, but I thought you might enjoy them today."

A Christmas coloring book? I quit coloring a long time ago. I preferred to draw. And if Aunt Susannah Hope thought Chesler would sit there and color elves and Christmas trees for more than three minutes without putting red and green marks on that white table, then she had another think coming.

I told her thank you and pinched the back of Chesler's arm. He yelped and when he looked at me, and I nodded toward Aunt Susannah Hope. He finally got it and thanked her too. I sat at one end of the table, and he sat down at the other end. He thumbed through the coloring book.

I knew he wouldn't color the elves or a doll. He didn't like cartoons or clowns, or anything that kinda looked human but wasn't. When a clown showed up at Gary Wilson's birthday party last summer, Chesler nearly took down the hedge running away. I didn't know about that boy. I guessed he just liked real people better.

He turned every page until he saw skates and a sled, then he started coloring and chattering away just like he did in the car last night. He went over his wish list again, and then he started singing.

I didn't want to color, but I did. It was the polite thing to do after getting mad about the birdcage, and Aunt Susannah Hope was trying to make us happy. She just didn't know I would rather draw a picture of Mama in my sketchbook.

All of a sudden Chesler stopped singing and put his crayon down. "Look, Kate." He jumped up, knocking his chair over on his way around the table to show me his picture. The little white Christmas tree, the one decorated with silver and gold balls on the window seat in the bay window? Well, it wasn't ready for a five-year-old boy, in his sock feet, flying around the table with a coloring book for wings.

I could see disaster coming. He bumped the table, hit the floor, and the coloring book went flying into the Christmas tree. Chesler's feet, the coloring book, and that Christmas tree went in three different directions. I got up to see if he was all right. He always cried when he fell no matter if he was hurt or not.

Aunt Susannah Hope ran to the Christmas tree and started picking up Christmas balls. Pieces of silver covered the floor, so I knew something was broken. She fussed at Chesler for being rowdy. "Chesler, why can't you learn to be careful?" My aunt didn't know that was like asking Granny Grace not to be bossy.

I helped him get up off the floor before he got into the broken pieces. He was crying because he was scared. I tried to tell him it was okay, but Aunt Susannah Hope just kept saying, "It is not okay. You knocked the tree over and broke two of the Christmas balls."

I picked him up and sat down in the chair, and he held on to me like a baby spider monkey. "Tell her you're sorry," I whispered in his ear. This was something else on Mama's list of things for me to do—make sure Chesler used good manners. But Chesler just kept holding on to me and whimpering. When Aunt Susannah finally got the tree back on the window seat, Chesler got out of my lap and knelt on the floor where my aunt was still picking up the pieces of the shattered silver ball.

"I'm sorry, Aunt Susannah Hope. I'm really sorry."

She shook her head. "You broke it. You broke it."

He tried to hug her. "I'm sorry I broke it, but I didn't broke your heart." I remembered what Mama used to say when we broke something: "It's okay. What you broke was just a thing and now it's a broken thing, but you didn't break my heart." After that always came a hug.

Chesler said it again about not breaking her heart.

Aunt Susannah Hope dropped the broken pieces on the floor and grabbed Chesler and gave him a big hug. She kept saying, "I'm sorry, Chesler. I'm so sorry." I thought she was. I thought she was sorry about a lot of things. She wasn't mean; she just didn't know how to be like Mama. Then she ran out of the kitchen to the bathroom.

Aunt Susannah probably had to breathe in her paper bag again, but I didn't care. All I wanted was to go home. I didn't want to color anymore. I didn't want to draw. I didn't want to hear any more of Chesler's stupid songs. I didn't want to watch Aunt Susannah Hope get her knickers in a twist about a white plastic Christmas tree with silver balls on it, and besides, it didn't even look real. Didn't she remember it was Christmas and Mama wasn't here? I just wanted to be at home, standing at the kitchen window, washing dishes and watching the redbird in the cedar tree.

CHAPTER NINE

*D*ADDY AND UNCLE Don didn't come home for lunch, but Granny Grace walked in just about the time we sat down to eat. Maybe she could smell Aunt Susannah Hope's barbecue and beans. My aunt didn't know much about children, but she knew a lot about good cooking, the kind that Daddy said would stick to your ribs.

Chesler wanted to ask the blessing before we ate. I gave him my look that said I'd pinch him if he did it wrong. Sometimes when he said the blessing, he used the one Uncle Luke taught him just to make Daddy laugh. "Good bread, good meat. Good Lord, let's eat. Amen."

But Chesler said a sweet blessing, saying he was sorry for messing up the Christmas tree, and even asking God to take care of Daddy and Uncle Don. I opened my eyes while he was praying, and Granny and Aunt Susannah Hope were smiling with their eyes closed.

After we'd been eating awhile, Granny Grace said, "Susannah Hope, you look a little green around the gills. Are you coming down with something?"

Aunt Susannah pushed the beans around on her plate like Chesler pushed around brussels sprouts when he didn't want to eat them. "I'm fine. I just haven't been outside lately with all this cold weather."

Granny Grace just said, "Uh huh" and looked like she was worried about something she wasn't saying. But she changed the subject. "Well, I like the Christmas plans you talked about this morning."

After Daddy and Uncle Don left this morning, I heard Aunt Susannah Hope talking to Granny on the phone. She told her all about Laramie, and then I heard her say, "I'm just plain weary of being sad, so I'm going to make a party out of the holidays starting today. I'm planning to do all the things Diana Joy would have done with Kate and Chesler if she were here."

I was thinking she had gotten off to a bad start on her plans. Mama would never have gotten so out of sorts about a plastic Christmas tree.

Then Granny changed the subject again. "Any news from John or Don?"

My aunt said, "Nothing yet. I hope they find her soon. I can't bear to think about that poor little girl out in the cold."

Granny and I had seconds. Lunch was so good, especially the potato salad, but Aunt Susannah Hope just kept pushing food around on her plate. I thought Chesler and I were just too much for her, and we had worn her out.

After lunch, Granny Grace made an announcement. "We're making PB and F before your aunt and I go upstairs to work on a project. And don't you ask me any questions about this project. You kids know it's getting close to Christmas." Then she winked. Granny always winked when she was up to something.

Chesler was getting whiny. "I don't want a peanut butter and jelly sandwich because I just had lunch."

Granny laughed. "No, we're making PB and F, pepper-mint bark and fudge, not PB and Js."

Nobody made fudge like Granny. Everybody told her she could start a business with that candy. She made a thick layer of dark chocolate fudge, and on top, she put a layer of white chocolate with crushed peppermint candy.

Now this was Aunt Susannah Hope's kitchen, but when Granny was there, she was in charge. She started passing out orders again like the parade marshal. "Susannah Hope, get all the ingredients out for me and bring me the biggest, heaviest pot you got." Granny was doing all the measuring and mixing. "Now, Kate, you stir when I put it all in the pot. Chesler, you and your aunt need to start breaking up the peppermint candy for the white chocolate."

Aunt Susannah put the peppermint candy pieces in a cloth bag and got the hammer and let Chesler go to work. He liked to hammer, and he was good at breaking things. Aunt Susannah Hope turned on the Christmas music, and Chesler hammered in rhythm to "Deck the Halls." The scent of chocolate and peppermint filled the kitchen, making it smell more like Christmas instead of dried-up flowers.

When the sugar and butter and chocolate and milk had boiled exactly eight minutes, I quit stirring and Granny Grace poured it out fast onto a pan and set it out on the back porch for a few minutes to cool. "Come here, Chesler. While the fudge is cooling, let's melt the white chocolate. You pour in the peppermint candy and stir it."

When the white chocolate was ready, I brought the fudge in for Granny to pour the peppermint bark on top.

Then I took it all back to the porch. Chesler stood at the window. Granny asked him, "What are you doing?"

"I'm guarding the PB and F."

"Guarding the candy? What on earth for?"

"Some bird or squirrel might try to get it."

"Birds and squirrels don't like chocolate and peppermint. Now it would be another story if we put my sugar-coated peanuts out there." Granny laughed at him.

Chesler didn't have much to worry about, but when he did worry, he worried about strange things. So he just kept standing there, his nose to the window. At least it kept him quiet for a while.

The hardest part of making that PB and F was waiting for it to cool so Granny could cut the first piece. It didn't take long because it was freezing outside. I thought about how fast that hot fudge cooled on the back porch, and then I thought about Laramie and how cold she might be wherever she was.

Granny cut us a little piece of fudge from the corner. Aunt Susannah Hope didn't want any. "Maybe I'll eat some on Christmas day. You know, I can't remember a Christmas without Granny's fudge."

"Me, either," Chesler piped in.

"That's right, all five Christmases of your life. Now listen to me, you two," Granny Grace said. "If you behave while Aunt Susannah and I work on the project upstairs, I'll slice up some so you can take it home with you tonight."

My aunt put on a Christmas movie for us to watch. It wasn't cowboys and Indians, but Chesler settled in to watch while I pulled out my sketchbook. I heard the creaks when Granny Grace and Aunt Susannah Hope climbed the stairs, and before long the hum of their sewing machines started.

Mama loved this old house where she grew up, with all its secret hiding places and stairs and closets. She told me one time it was over a hundred years old, and that's why it moaned and groaned like Grandpa getting up out of his chair after a nap.

After Aunt Susannah Hope bought the house from Granny and Grandpa, she and Mama used the second floor to run their sewing business. Mama could design things, and they both could really sew. They made curtains and pillows and dresses and anything else the rich ladies in town could think of. And when they weren't sewing for somebody else, my aunt made things to decorate her house, and Mama sewed dresses for me. I missed picking out fabrics and patterns with her, and modeling the finished product, twirling in front of a mirror while she smiled.

One day last summer before Mama got sick, I read upstairs while they sewed. Mama and Aunt Susannah Hope started chatting about how when they were girls they made secret hiding places for their treasures. They would stick things behind loose boards in closets and under the shelves in cabinets. I was tired of reading and decided to look for some of their secret places. It didn't take long to find one of their treasures, a note stuck with chewing gum underneath a bookshelf. I brought it to Mama, and her eyes lit up. "It's a love note to that boy I had a crush on in fifth grade!" she laughed after she read it. "We even got into your granny's reddest lipstick so I could seal that note with a kiss."

"Can I keep it?" I asked. I could hardly believe Mama had been a girl my age. This was proof.

"Okay, but you'll have to hide it again." She handed me a stick of gum and winked. "You know what to do."

When I got back home, I chewed the gum then stuck the note to the bottom of my desk drawer with the gum. It was still there, my own hidden treasure. Thinking of it now, I tried to draw Mama's lips in my sketchbook, just to help me remember.

Then I remembered another treasure. Once when I was nine, I was poking around Granny Grace's old sewing chest, with its pull-out drawer that held spools of thread. I opened the top drawer and found an old envelope. Inside was a strand of hair tied in pink ribbon.

"What's this?" I asked Granny Grace, holding it up for her to see.

"Oh, that," she laughed. "That's one of my favorite treasures. I once cut a lock from your mama's hair when she was a little girl so I'd have her with me forever."

Forever came too soon. But Granny's treasure gave me an idea for Mama's Christmas present.

Those sewing machines hummed all afternoon. Chesler watched fifteen minutes of the Christmas movie before he fell asleep, and I worked on my drawings in my sketchbook. I liked being in that old house and thinking about all its treasures and especially Granny's treasure. I could see Mama, and I could almost see her running around this house when she was a little girl, when it didn't have white furniture and dead flowers and so much stuff to break.

It was nearly dark when Daddy and Uncle Don finally came through the front door, their faces looking like

Pastor Simmons did just before he preached, all serious like. They would have been smiling and talking if they had found Laramie. Daddy said, "Go gather your things. We need to get home because Uncle Luke's coming."

Now Chesler always forgot to brush his teeth, but he didn't forget what Granny Grace said about taking some PB and F home with us. So he went yelling and running up the stairs for Granny. She and Aunt Susannah Hope came down the stairs and started asking Daddy and Uncle Don more questions than my teacher asks on review day. Daddy just said Uncle Don could fill them in after we left. That meant Daddy didn't want to talk about it, and he didn't want us to hear about it.

Daddy didn't say a word 'til we got home. He hadn't slept all night and all day, and he had been out in the cold too. He looked like he used to look when Mama was real sick and he was taking care of her, only his face was red from the cold. After building a fire he headed straight for the shower. "Kate, you and Chesler take care of Uncle Luke if he gets here before I get cleaned up."

Daddy was coming back down the stairs when Uncle Luke barreled through the front door. He looked like a younger version of Daddy, tall and lanky with straight, brown hair and brown eyes. Daddy hugged him and snatched off his cap. "When in the world are you getting a haircut? We don't want any shaggy-haired doctors in this family."

Uncle Luke hugged him again. "Maybe I'll get my haircut when I smell chili cooking. All I smell around here are Chesler's stinky feet." Then he grabbed Chesler and swung him over his shoulders. Chesler screamed and giggled.

"No chili tonight. I gotta make good on my promise to Chesler and Kate. I promised them waffles for breakfast, but I was called out to work in the middle of the night."

With Uncle Luke helping, we had hot eggs and hot waffles at the same time. Daddy didn't say a word about Laramie and what he had been doing all day.

After supper Uncle Luke helped me with the dishes. It was too dark to see the redbird even if she was in the cedar tree. When we all got to the den, Daddy stoked the fire, and Chesler put on a show like he always did when Uncle Luke came home, singing everything he knew and telling him all about his Christmas list.

Then Uncle Luke told Daddy about all the stuff he was learning in medical school. That's when Chesler fell asleep on his blanket in front of the fire. I listened for a little while, and then I pretended to be asleep. Grown-ups talked different when they thought children were asleep.

Daddy asked, "So are you going to see Lisa Applegate while you're home?"

"Yes, I do plan to see her. We've been talking almost every day since I was home for Diana Joy's funeral."

"Sounds serious," Daddy joked.

But he didn't ask any more questions or tease, so Uncle Luke said, "Okay, big brother, cough it up. What's on your mind?"

"We got a little girl missing, Laramie Fields." Daddy told him about Laramie and her dad and what happened the night before. "We searched the area all around the house and into the woods but didn't find anything. The snow covered up all the clues. The police are bringing in some dogs to help with the hunt tonight."

Uncle Luke got up. "You go get some sleep. I'll join the search."

"But you just got home. You must be tired."

"I'm used to pulling all-nighters. I'll be fine."

Daddy didn't even try to talk him out of it. "Okay, if you're up to it, I know the guys will appreciate the help. I'll sleep for a few hours and get Grace to take the kids. I'll take your place in the search at daybreak."

Uncle Luke left, and Daddy fell asleep on the sofa. So I just stayed quiet 'til the fire went out. Chesler would get cold on the floor without the fire, so I woke him up and told him we were going to bed. I covered Daddy up with Chesler's blanket and took Chesler to his room. Another night without brushing his teeth.

Good. It was quiet. Daddy was downstairs, Chesler was asleep, and I could finally pull out my sketchbook. I turned on my desk light and took my pencils out and started to draw. I was thinking about Mama and Laramie's mama. Mama loved us and wanted to stay, and she told me about faith and family and forever. I knew Mama wasn't coming back no matter how much I wanted her to, but I knew I'd see her again. But Laramie's mom? I wondered why she never told Laramie where she was going and why she didn't take Laramie with her if she could.

I didn't have my mama very long, but I was glad I got to say good-bye to her. I began to sketch her face, and just as I was drawing her eyelashes something tapped against the window. I looked up. Probably the tree limb tapping again. I looked at the clock. Nearly midnight. I had been drawing for a long time.

I closed my eyes, trying to remember how Mama's eyelashes really looked. Her picture was too small to tell. Tap, tap again. This time I got up to look, and something hit the window right in front of my face. I jumped back, then I stepped to the window again to see. There on the ground underneath the elm tree, I thought I saw someone waving at me. My breath had already fogged up the window, so I rubbed the windowpane with my pajama sleeve before I peered out.

It was a person. Somebody was standing in the snow waving at me. I knew it couldn't be, but I hoped it was Mama.

Chapter Ten

I PUSHED AND PUSHED on the window. The cold wind blew right in my face when I finally got the window open enough to stick my head outside. I wasn't seeing things. There was a person, all bundled up and leaning against the tree. I couldn't tell who it was. But whoever it was knew my name and was calling me. It was kind of a hoarse whisper, sort of like the person couldn't talk any louder or maybe didn't want anybody else to hear. I still couldn't tell who it was, so I asked, "Who's there?"

"It's me. Laramie." Then she slumped to the ground.

I flew out of my room and took the stairs three at a time 'til I got to the bottom. Laramie. Laramie was here, and she was alive. I ran out the front door and knelt beside her. She was a puddle of coat and blanket underneath that elm tree. When I tried to wake her up, she opened her eyes and closed them again. I tried to pull her arm to get her up. She was limp like my rag doll. She wouldn't wake up. She just didn't have enough strength.

I ran in the house hollering for Daddy. "Get up, get up, Daddy. It's Laramie. She's here."

"You having a bad dream, little peep?" Then he really woke up and saw I was shivering because I had been outside.

"It's not a dream, Daddy. Laramie is outside in the front yard, but I can't get her up."

Daddy's eyes widened, and he leaped off the couch. When we got to the front door, I pointed under the elm tree. Without even putting his shoes on, Daddy headed out the door. Moving fast was nothing new to Daddy. He was used to ambulances and emergencies and sirens, and I think his own siren was blaring inside.

In moments Daddy picked up that bundle, and had Laramie lying on the sofa before I could lock the door. "Go, Kate, go get all the blankets you can find, and don't waste time doing it." Daddy was checking her pulse as I reached the bottom of the stairs.

I grabbed the comforter on Daddy's bed and the extra quilt in his closet. Daddy was talking to somebody on the phone when I got back downstairs. "Yeah, her pulse is slow but steady. I will." He hung up.

"That was Uncle Luke. He's on his way back home." Daddy put his fingers back on Laramie's neck and checked her pulse again. "Here, put the quilt down and help me." Daddy lifted Laramie up and asked me to take off her coat. "Good, all her clothes are dry. That's a sign she's had shelter."

Her lips were blue with cold, and her hair was bloody and matted to her head. "You want me to go run a hot tub of water?"

"No, it's too dangerous to heat the body that fast. I want Luke to take a look at her first."

Daddy kept calling Laramie's name, and sometimes she would open her eyes and look at him, then close them again. I took off her shoes and socks so Daddy could look at her toes. He had already looked at her fingers. "No frostbite. That's good," Daddy said.

I sat right beside her and rubbed her arm while Daddy went to the truck to get his medical bag. He was checking Laramie's temperature when Uncle Luke walked in with a police officer. "Kate, go to the kitchen and pour Laramie a glass of juice."

Now how was Laramie supposed to drink juice if she was asleep? I think Daddy just wanted me to leave the room. As I opened the refrigerator and pulled out the pitcher of juice, I heard Daddy say to Uncle Luke and the officer, "She appears to have a mild case of hypothermia, and she's dehydrated, plus she's got a bad gash on her forehead. I think we'd better get her to the hospital. They'll give her some fluids and check out that cut on her head."

"I think you're right," Uncle Luke said. "Just take my truck. It's warm, and it'll be better than calling an ambulance this late. I'll stay with the kids."

The policeman said, "She's in good hands, so I'll head back to the station to make a report and call off the search." I heard his footsteps cross the floor and the front door close behind him.

Daddy was putting on his shoes when I came back with the juice. "Thanks, honey, but I think we'd better take Laramie to the hospital now." Daddy grabbed his coat and picked Laramie up off the sofa. Uncle Luke held the door, and Daddy and Laramie disappeared into the night.

Since Laramie was gone, I gave Uncle Luke the juice, and he smiled at me a little and drank it down. "Thanks, Kate. I needed that." He laid a warm hand on my shoulder. "You must be someone Laramie trusts for her to have come here like that. I'm proud of you."

"Is she going to be okay?" I asked.

"She'll be fine. Your daddy wanted to be sure she had the very best care. Now, you'd better get back to bed. I just need a hot shower, and then I'm going to bed too."

Uncle Luke headed for the bathroom, and the house was quiet again. I went to my room. It was freezing 'cause the window was still open. So I closed it, turned out the light, and climbed into bed. With the blanket pulled up tight under my chin, I prayed, "Thank You, God, for taking care of Laramie and for bringing Daddy and Uncle Luke home safe. Oh, and thank You, God, for keeping Laramie warm enough to stay alive. Amen."

Then I remembered I hadn't put a smiley-face on my calendar tonight. I didn't think long about who smiled because of me today. Today deserved the biggest smile ever, because Laramie was safe. I got up, turned on the light, and drew a huge smiley face on a yellow dot, then put it on December 19. Less than a week 'til Christmas and I still didn't know how to get a present to heaven, but Laramie was living proof God answered prayer. Maybe He would get Mama's Christmas present to her too.

When I woke up Tuesday morning, I heard talking in the kitchen. Daddy was home, and Uncle Luke was cooking breakfast. Uncle Luke was a better cook than Daddy because he never had a wife to cook for him. After their parents got killed in a car wreck, Uncle Luke, who was just seventeen, had to cook because Daddy was doing everything else to take care of things.

I dressed and went downstairs. I stood in the den and listened for a minute because I knew Daddy would stop talking if I went in the kitchen. Then I wouldn't know a thing.

"Guess the police chief was full of Christmas spirit because he brought Fields to the hospital last night for a supervised visit. Fields acted so grateful she had been found, and he kept telling her how everything was going to change. He told her that her mother was alive, and he hoped she would be coming home."

"Where was she?" Uncle Luke asked.

"Staying with her sister in upstate New York. Apparently the marriage was on the rocks, and she left to clear her head and get some help with a drinking problem. She wrote to Laramie, but Fields never gave her the letters, for fear of losing his daughter too."

"Unforgivable," Uncle Luke muttered.

"Who knows why people do the crazy things they do?" Daddy said. "But Fields seems to have had a huge wake-up call. He couldn't stop shaking my hand, telling me how grateful he was for taking care of his daughter."

I walked loud across the wood floor to the kitchen so they'd hear me coming, and they wouldn't think I was snooping around just to hear what they were saying.

After hugs and good mornings, Daddy made me a cup of hot chocolate and poured himself a cup of coffee. Then we sat down at the table while Uncle Luke sifted the flour. Daddy acted like I was a grown-up and just started talking. "Laramie's doing well." Then he started asking me all these questions about how I knew Laramie was outside last night.

"Well, I was in my room, but I wasn't asleep good yet. She threw something at my window to get my attention."

I didn't tell them I was sitting at my desk drawing. I didn't figure that was important for them to know.

"Why did she come here of all places?" Daddy asked. "Were you especially nice to her at school?"

I shook my head. "Not really. But I have been talking to her more lately." I didn't say why—that Laramie was the only kid in my class who knew what it felt like to not have a mama.

Uncle Luke just kept cooking while we talked. Nothing smelled better than bacon frying in the morning.

"Why did Laramie run away?" I asked.

"Well, she told the sheriff that she got scared because she saw her daddy's friends had drugs. And when she told her daddy to ask them to leave, they had a big argument. She was so scared and mad that she just ran away. Apparently she hid in a shed behind the school."

"That must be the shed where the janitor keeps the bird food. She volunteers all the time to fill up the feeders."

Daddy put his coffee cup down. "Thankfully she had mind enough to bring a snack and a bottle of water and a blanket with her. Said she planned to stay just long enough to get even with her dad and then go back home. But she was scared of how he'd react to her running away, so she came here instead."

It didn't sound like the whole story to me. "But if she just ran away, how did she get hurt?"

Daddy shook his head. "She said she ran into a tree limb in the dark."

Uncle Luke pointed the fork he was using to turn the bacon straight at Daddy. "And do you believe her or do you think she's covering for her dad?"

"I think she's telling the truth. She had a pretty good gash on her head that could have been made by a limb. She said she slept a lot, so she may have even had a slight concussion from it, which is why she didn't come to us sooner. Her dad has a pretty bad temper, but I don't think he'd hurt her like that."

I looked at Daddy. "I think she came here because one time I told her you were a paramedic, and she knew you could help her."

"What happens now?" Uncle Luke asked, shooting a glance at me like he wasn't sure the answer was one I would be allowed to hear.

Daddy sipped his coffee. "They're keeping her at the hospital for a day or two because she has nowhere else to go. She certainly can't go home by herself. The police are trying to find somebody to take care of her 'til they can get her daddy cleared or they can find her mama."

Uncle Luke turned off the stove. "Why don't we bring her here? We could all take care of her."

Daddy nodded slowly. "Don and Susannah were cleared to become foster parents recently. Laramie just might be the perfect trial run for them. No diapers or middle-of-the-night feedings. And she knows Kate, so Kate can go over and keep her company."

Uncle Luke said, "Good idea. A female touch may be what's needed here."

What with Aunt Susannah Hope's hovering, and her disliking ruckuses, and having to breathe in a paper bag all the time, I wasn't so sure she was ready for taking care of Laramie. And I knew Laramie was not ready for Aunt Susannah Hope. Laramie knew how to be nice, but as Granny would say, "She could be a handful." I knew sass and bad words would never be at home at my aunt's house. But I didn't say anything.

All the talking about Laramie was done when Daddy went to get Chesler for breakfast. We had scrambled eggs and crispy bacon and real hash browns, not the kind that came out of the freezer looking like a deck of Skip-Bo cards dipped in grated potatoes.

After breakfast Daddy went up to take a shower and Chesler went to his room to dress. Uncle Luke started to collect the dishes, but I said, "Dishwashing's my job, Uncle Luke, especially since you made real potatoes."

I should have taken a good look at that kitchen before I volunteered, though. Pots and pans and spills and scraps of potatoes and eggshells were everywhere. I didn't know you could mess up so many dishes just cooking breakfast for four people.

Uncle Luke helped me get things stacked up at the sink and took out the trash. Then he poured himself another cup of coffee and went to the den to read the newspaper, leaving me to do the dishes.

Mama left me a whole list about how to wash the dishes. Now when Daddy washed the dishes, he just grabbed whatever was closest to the sink and started washing, but I liked to do it the way Mama said, and I didn't even have to look at the list anymore. With the sink full of hot water just covered in suds, I started with the juice glasses and the coffee cups. Mama said, "No greasy smudges if you wash them first."

I was scraping egg off the plates when my friend the redbird lit in the cedar tree. She balanced herself on that limb and stretched her wings, soaking up the winter morning sunshine. Reminded me of Granny stretching and rubbing her arms in front of a warm fire. Then the redbird sat and chirped like she was talking to me. If I could chirp back, I'd tell her how pretty she was and how I wished I could touch her and how glad I was that Laramie was safe.

CHAPTER ELEVEN

*A*FTER DADDY SHOWERED, he stirred up a pot of chili in the crock-pot. Then he told me, "I'm meeting Granny Grace over at Aunt Susannah Hope's. Your Uncle Luke's here to take care of you."

I was glad to hear that we could stay home, and Uncle Luke and Chesler could do boy things while I finished my drawings. But right before Daddy walked out the door, he said, "Luke, how about taking the kids out to the woods and cutting a few holly branches? Grace wanted us to put some red berries in the garland on the staircase, and I haven't gotten around to it."

"Translated, that means you don't want her to come over here and see that you haven't been following orders." Uncle Luke laughed.

"You got it!" Daddy headed out the door.

"Ches-ler! Katy J!" Uncle Luke almost sang our names. "Report to the kitchen for duty."

Chesler barreled down the steps with mismatched clothes on, holding his shoes and socks. He hadn't brushed his hair, and it was still in swirls like somebody had pin-curled it and had just taken the clips out.

"Put on your shoes, and get your coats. We're going holly hunting." Uncle Luke lifted the lid off the chili and gave it a stir.

"Who's Holly? Is that another little girl who got lost?"

Uncle Luke smiled and winked at me. "No, red top, holly like holly berries. Your granny wants holly berries in the cedar garland. And we all know we do what Granny Grace says, right?"

"Yeah, if you do, you get chocolate fudge with peppermint. And quit calling me red top. That's Granny Grace's rooster."

"Fudge sounds like a good enough reason for me to do what she says." Uncle Luke zipped up his coat and put on his hat.

"Coats on?"

"Yes, sir." Chesler and I saluted and said it together like Uncle Luke taught us a long time ago.

"And zipped?"

"Yes, sir."

"Gloves on?"

"Yes, sir."

"Ears covered?"

"Can't hear you!" Chesler giggled and grabbed Uncle Luke around his thighs.

"Good, then let's go. Nothing like Kentucky woods in December."

The snow had hardened overnight, crunching under our feet. Uncle Luke made a game out of stepping in his footprints in the snow.

I didn't want to cut the holly at the edge of the woods because I wanted to leave it for the redbird. I was scared she'd go away if she didn't have some berries. So when Uncle Luke pulled out his clippers at the first bush he came to, I said, "Hey, Chesler, wouldn't it be fun if Uncle Luke took us on an adventure in the woods?"

"Yeah, yeah, a real adventure!" Chesler tried to jump up and down in the snow.

"Yeah, Uncle Luke, let's do it. We got our tracks right here in the snow if we get lost."

Uncle Luke agreed and took off at a quick pace like he was daring us to keep up. He took big steps sometimes and little steps sometimes and then sideways steps. Chesler kept falling down trying to keep up, or maybe he was just falling on purpose to make Uncle Luke laugh. When we got to a holly tree with berries, Uncle Luke snipped and put the branches in the baskets Chesler and I had.

As we headed back, I said to Uncle Luke, "Granny Grace asked me and Chesler what we were planning to give Baby Jesus for His birthday this year. She told us about the shepherds and the wise men and the gifts they gave."

Chesler piped in. "Yeah, the shepherds gave the baby a lamb, and He didn't even need one."

"Well, I don't think the baby needing something is the point, Chesler." Uncle Luke kept walking, and we tried to keep up.

"Yeah, but if we get Baby Jesus something for His birthday and all, how do we get it to Him? I mean, how do you get something to heaven?" I was nearly out of breath from walking so fast to keep up with Uncle Luke, but I wanted to hear his answer.

Uncle Luke smiled. "Good question. I think what your granny meant is that you can give something to somebody who needs it, and it's like giving it to Jesus."

"You mean, somebody else gets His present?"

"Oh, He'll know all about how you gave something to somebody in need, but He won't get the present. He's in heaven, remember?"

"But how do I get a present to heaven?"

I was disappointed when Uncle Luke's beeper went off, but he probably didn't know the answer to my question anyway. He fished it off his belt and looked at it. "Gotta get back to the house to make a call." Whoever beeped him put a big smile on his face and made him walk even faster. "We just might be having someone special over for lunch today."

"I know. It's Miss Applegate."

"Yep, you got it. If I had a prize, I'd give it to you."

"So can I call Miss Applegate 'Miss Lisa' when she's at our house? She said I could last time."

"You call her Miss Applegate until she asks you to call her Miss Lisa. Then it's okay, but don't ask."

Chesler butted in. "We saw you kissing Miss Applegate once out behind the barn at Granny's. Are you gonna marry her?"

"Well, that's a big question coming from such a small bundle of red coat and blue mittens. Do you think I should?"

"Yeah, yeah. She's real pretty, and she makes good peanut butter and jelly sandwiches in shapes. She made me one that looked like an Indian teepee. And she stuck some pretzels together with peanut butter to look like a campfire."

"Well, if she can do all that, maybe I should think about marrying her." He smiled big. "But John Chesler Harding Junior, if you mention this to Miss Applegate, then I'm going to make you watch cartoons until New Year's, do you hear?"

"That means zip it, Chesler," I told him. "No more talk about Uncle Luke and Miss Applegate getting married. That's none of your business." Then I turned to Uncle Luke. "But I think you should marry her too, Uncle Luke. She looks at you the way Mama looked at Daddy. That's all I have to say." Then I zipped it.

Uncle Luke smiled, and we kept walking. When we got to the back porch, he grabbed an empty bucket before we went inside. "Okay, give me the baskets of holly and you two hang up your coats and junk. I'll put these branches in some water until Lisa gets here. Maybe she can help us figure out how to put this holly in the garland."

That wasn't all I hoped she would do. I had to figure out a way to get her to my room so she could see what I was drawing for Granny Grace and Aunt Susannah Hope. And maybe she would know how to get a present to heaven. So far nobody knew, not Pastor Simmons, not Emily, not Uncle Luke. And I didn't want to ask Daddy, because he'd just get sad.

Uncle Luke said he needed to get cleaned up. I knew why. Miss Applegate. Good. He'd be busy for a while, and Chesler could entertain himself. I'd get my drawings ready for Miss Applegate to see.

A half hour later Miss Applegate rang the doorbell. Uncle Luke sent me to answer it. Usually she dressed like a bouncy cheerleader, wearing jeans and a T-shirt and her long hair up high in a ponytail. But when I opened the door, Miss Applegate looked all grown up. She had on a long red coat made of wool, and when she took off her coat, she had on black slacks and boots and a black sweater with sparkly red and green Christmas balls on it. Her blonde hair hung down over her shoulders, and her blue eyes looked like two of Daddy's keepsake marbles.

I took her coat and hung it on the hall tree, and we stood at the bottom of the stairs, chatting. I knew the second Uncle Luke was at the top of the stairs even though I hadn't heard him. Her eyes lit up, and her bright red lips spread out all across her face. Uncle Luke bounded down the stairs and hugged her with both arms like Daddy used to hug Mama, and I think if I weren't there, Uncle Luke would have had red lipstick all across his face.

We sat at the table and had the hot chocolate Uncle Luke made, and then he asked Miss Applegate to help us with the holly.

"Okay, we'll need wire. Do you have some?"

"I'll check in John's tools." When Uncle Luke went to the garage to look for the wire, I told Miss Applegate I wanted to show her something upstairs but she had to keep it a secret. Uncle Luke came back in, and she said, "Shh, we'll go look later."

Uncle Luke grabbed the basket of holly and followed her to the stairs. The two of them, standing on the steps, poking those holly stems in the cedar garland, looked like they belonged in a Christmas movie. And when she poked herself with the wire, Uncle Luke rushed off for medicine and acted like she had cut her finger off. He doctored and bandaged it and then kissed it. They were in love. Even I could see that.

Uncle Luke went off to set the table for lunch and that was my chance. I grabbed Miss Applegate and pulled her toward the stairs. "Uncle Luke," I called. "I have to show Miss Applegate one of my projects up in my room. We'll only be a minute."

My sketchbook was on my desk and the two photographs of Mama were lying on top. Miss Applegate looked at the photos first, and when she opened my sketchbook, she couldn't believe it when I showed her the pictures I drew of Mama. She had to sit down on the bed to look at them. She really studied the first one before she turned the page to the next one. Nothing, not one word, came out of her mouth.

I stood beside her. "I don't want to forget how Mama looked. But look how the pictures are all smeary."

"Smeary is okay. The drawings are beautiful, Kate." She hugged me. "And you're never going to forget how lovely your mother was. Your eyes and your heart will remember, and now your hands and fingers will remember too because you're drawing her."

"But I don't know how to keep the drawings from smearing."

"What if I take them home with me and do something to make sure they won't? And I'm pretty certain I have a couple of extra frames for them, as well. Would you like that?"

"I'd really like that. Then I can keep it a surprise from everybody. If I don't have to get frames, I won't even have to tell Daddy." I watched her close the sketchbook. "Miss Applegate?"

"Hey, Kate, don't you remember? It's okay to call me Miss Lisa when we're at your house."

"Thank you, ma'am, Miss Lisa. Can I ask you a question?"

"What question?" Uncle Luke showed up at the doorway just then, with a look on his face like—if you ask her that question I told you not to ask, you'll be in this yellow room on bread and water until the snow thaws.

I turned to him. "I was hoping Miss Lisa might know how to get a present to heaven by Christmas. You remember what Granny said."

"A present to heaven? By Christmas?" Miss Lisa looked at Uncle Luke. "Oh, my goodness."

That meant she didn't know. "It's okay, it's a hard question. You don't have to answer it." I didn't tell her that nobody else I asked knew the answer either.

"Daddy's home." Chesler's voice was like a trumpet all the way up the stairs.

"Coming!" Uncle Luke walked over and held out his hand to Miss Lisa. "Come on, you two artístes. It's almost lunchtime, and that tub of chili's smelling real good."

Uncle Luke was right, Daddy's chili smelled real good. Everybody was so hungry Daddy skipped making the corn bread and got out the box of saltines. Next thing I knew, Uncle Luke and Daddy were passing out bowls and crackers and root beer like it was the soup kitchen down at the Methodist Church.

Once we were settled at the table, Daddy asked Chesler if he wanted to say the blessing. Mistake. He didn't say the one Uncle Luke taught him, but he thanked God for every person in our family by name, and then he thanked God for our house, and for the Christmas tree and for the bowls of chili, and when he started telling God he hoped Miss Applegate would marry Uncle Luke, Daddy interrupted and said, "Amen."

From what I heard Daddy telling Uncle Luke, Chesler should have been praying for Laramie. She didn't have anything on Chesler's list she could thank God for, and she had nowhere to go, because Uncle Don and Aunt Susannah Hope had said no to taking her in.

CHAPTER TWELVE

*C*AT THE LUNCH table Miss Lisa said she was going Christmas shopping that afternoon and asked Uncle Luke to go with her. He just sat there and didn't say a word. I jabbed him in the ribs with my elbow, and he looked at me funny before turning back to her. "What would you think about catching a movie later because I have some shopping to do myself?" Then he wiggled his eyebrows like he did when he tried to be funny or cute.

Lucky for him she said, "Okay."

I made sure to give her my sketchbook before she left. When I was hugging her good-bye, she whispered, "I'll get them framed and wrapped, and you'll have them under the tree on Christmas morning." I thanked her and hugged her again real tight.

Daddy pulled on the sleeve of my sweater. "So what's all the whispering about?"

Before I could answer him, Miss Lisa said, "It's Christmas, John. The season of peace and joy and secrets. So don't ask." She gave Daddy a hug and walked out on the porch with Uncle Luke right behind to see her off.

I wished I could hear what they were saying, but Daddy marched Chesler and me back to the kitchen. "Dishwashing time, Kate. I washed up the big nasty stuff and just left you the glasses and bowls."

"Thanks, Daddy."

He sent Chesler to the den and told him to watch a video. "Kate, what are you doing this afternoon?"

"I don't know. Sounds like Uncle Luke won't be here. You gotta work?"

"Nope, not today. What would you say about you and me going to the hospital to visit Laramie? Maybe we can get Uncle Luke to take Chesler with him shopping."

"Or maybe we can leave him at Aunt Susannah Hope's." I liked the idea of leaving Chesler somewhere else for a while, but I couldn't tell Daddy I didn't want to go to the hospital. Not that I didn't want to see Laramie, but the last time I went to the hospital, Mama was there.

"Your aunt is not up to it today, so we'll count on Uncle Luke. I think Laramie would like it a whole lot if we came to see her. She's in that hospital room all by herself. I called Pastor Simmons and asked him to stop by and see her, but that's not the same as seeing somebody she really knows."

"Okay. Maybe I should make her a card before we go."

"Great idea, daughter. How'd you get to be so thoughtful?" Daddy smiled and walked out of the kitchen.

I was rinsing the glasses when the redbird lit in the cedar tree. I looked at that redbird, just wishing I had a camera so I could take a picture. Only five more days 'til Christmas, and then maybe I'd have one.

I finished the dishes and went to my room. It took a little while to draw the picture on the card, and then I had to color it with pencils because I was almost out of paint. Maybe I should have asked for more paint for Christmas.

Daddy and Uncle Luke were talking at the kitchen table when I came back downstairs. Chesler was still watching the video and playing with his Matchbox cars, so I just sat down on the sofa with my card pretending to watch too, but I was really listening to Daddy and Uncle Luke talk.

Daddy sighed. "Yeah, Susannah Hope's just not up to taking Laramie right now. We may need to bring the girl here for a few days until they release her dad or they find her mother."

"Okay by me."

"I wish you'd check on Susannah while you're here, Luke. When I was over there this morning, she was pale and listless, and just didn't have much energy. I don't like that look. Reminded me of—"

He didn't finish his sentence, but I knew who he meant. Mama.

"Don't go jumping to conclusions. I mean, I can see why you would, but what Diana Joy had is not necessarily hereditary. I'll check on Susannah. The best I can do is to persuade her to see her own doctor."

"Just tell her I asked you to stop by. Think you can do it on your way to town to do your shopping this afternoon?"

Uncle Luke was sounding like a real doctor. "All right, if you insist."

"Thanks, Luke, just want your medical opinion. Now, little brother, when are you going to buy that sweet Lisa Applegate a ring? I think you've strung her along long enough."

"You don't have any problem saying what you think, do you, big brother?"

Daddy ignored him and just went on. "You're about to finish school. Now's the time to buy Lisa a ring before somebody else puts one on her finger."

"I don't know, John. I was thinking of waiting till I was done with my residency. I hear the hours are long."

"Well, why not just wait till you're fifty-two?"

"But, John, I mean...this a big decision."

"Look, Luke, take it from me. Don't waste one day. I'd give all I have for one more day with Diana Joy. You know you love Lisa, and she loves you. You're so good for each other. Well shoot, we all love her. Just buy the bloomin' ring and ask her to marry you."

"I hear you. But how can I be sure she's the one?"

"Simple. Three questions. Do you think about her all the time?"

"Well, mostly, when I'm not in class or studying for a serious exam."

"Do you think about anyone else more than you think about her?"

"No, I don't even think about anybody else except you and the kids and maybe a couple of my professors."

"Okay then, can you imagine your life without her?"

"Now, that you ask it like that, no, I can't."

"You're as sure as anyone ever can be, Luke. Just do it." I heard chairs scraping along the floor as they pushed back from the table. "I'm taking Kate to the hospital this afternoon to visit Laramie. Could you watch Chesler for an hour before you shop?"

"Sure thing."

Steps crossed the floor, and I buried my head in my book, pretending like I hadn't been paying any attention to them. Here I was again, hearing things I wasn't supposed to hear and having to keep it all to myself. Now I knew Aunt Susannah Joy was sick and Uncle Luke wanted to marry Miss Lisa, and I couldn't talk to anybody about it because I wasn't supposed to know.

Daddy came into the den. "Ready to go?"

"Just a minute, Daddy. Let me finish this page first." I said that so he wouldn't think I had been listening.

"Well, excuse me for interrupting." Daddy pinched my toe when he walked by the sofa. "Read it in a hurry. We need to get to the hospital. Uncle Luke's staying with Chesler, and we can't be gone long because he's still got shopping to do."

I set aside my book. "Okay, then. I'm ready. I'll get my coat." Before we left, I showed Daddy the card I made. He liked it.

When we drove past Aunt Susannah Hope's on our way to the hospital, I asked Daddy why Chesler couldn't stay there.

"Your aunt's a little under the weather."

"Yes, sir, she didn't eat her lunch yesterday, and she didn't look too good. I thought it was because Chesler and I are just too much for her. She's not like Mama."

"Nope, nobody's like your mama. She was one of a kind."

I was hoping Daddy would say something else about Aunt Susannah Hope so I could get rid of that secret. But he didn't. Daddy must have thought she was bad sick, and Daddy didn't like to talk about bad things.

"What would you think, little peep, about bringing Laramie home with us for a few days, maybe just through Christmas?"

"You mean all the way through Christmas Day?"

"Well, yes, she can't go home until they release her daddy, and she doesn't have relatives around these parts. So she has nowhere else to go, and I don't think we'd feel good about her being in a shelter for Christmas when we have a big house and family to share."

"But where will she sleep?"

"Oh, I thought she could share your room. Uncle Luke's home, so we can't put her in his bedroom."

I nodded. "This could be our birthday present to Baby Jesus, taking care of Laramie."

"You sound like your mama. That'll be a great present. Then let's ask Laramie when we get to the hospital. That'll make her feel better than any medicine. But I need to check on one thing at the hospital before we ask her, okay?"

"Yes, sir."

We stopped at the nurse's station so Daddy could talk to Dr. Rushing. Daddy told me to go down the hall and sit in the family waiting area until he finished talking to the doctor.

I remembered this room from when Mama was sick. It was uncomfortable and sad looking then, and nothing had changed. There were gray chairs and a gray floor, and three tables with old magazines and only one window. It was always cold, even in the summer when I had to sit in here and wait for Daddy. And it smelled like medicine or cleaning stuff.

I was just sitting there, squinching my eyes like that would get rid of my sad memories about being here with Mama, when I heard footsteps. I looked up, hoping I'd see Daddy, but it was an old man, older than Granny Grace.

He was standing right next to me in front of the table. His old gray coat almost touched the floor and looked like he had been wearing it forever, and his white hair poked out from under his wool cap. He coughed, cleared his throat, and said, "Mind if I sit here, little one?"

Now Mama and Daddy always taught me not to talk to strangers, but he didn't seem much like a stranger, and besides, I could outrun him to the door. "No, sir, it's okay," I said.

When he took off his gloves, I noticed they were old and worn like Daddy's work gloves. He took off his wool cap and stuffed his gloves and his cap in his coat pocket, and then he brushed his long white hair back and smoothed it down. That's when I saw his wrinkled face. His eyebrows looked like the bristles on a worn-out toothbrush, and his eyelids sagged a little bit like they were tired. His eyes were big and round and kinda gray and blue.

He had a quiet, kind voice, just like my grandpa's used to be. He unbuttoned his coat and sat down. That's when I noticed he wasn't dressed so good, and Granny Grace would have sent him straight to the shower before he could sit on her sofa or come to the table. I could see he was holding something under his arm inside his coat. It looked like books, but I wasn't sure. He kept his distance, and I was glad.

Surely Daddy would be here in a minute, but I thought I should say something. "Are you visiting somebody?" I asked.

"Well, you might say that."

I didn't know what to make of that, so I just said, "I used to come here a lot when my mama was sick, but today I'm visiting my friend. That is, when my daddy comes to take me to see her."

"Well, I'd say that's a mighty nice thing you're doing, visiting your friend." He fumbled under his coat and brought out a bright green book of matches out of the pocket of his ratty-looking sweater. I could read the words Haven of Hope printed in gold on the front before he started twirling it through his fingers. "It's a good thing to have friends. Now take me, I just mostly move around making new friends. But I find moving around is a good way to meet folks, just like meeting you here today."

"Yes, sir." He seemed nice, so I thought it was okay to keep talking to him. "We're taking care of my friend Laramie during the holidays. She's all by herself. Her mama's gone, and her daddy's in jail. I don't know if I was supposed to tell you all that, but anyway, I told Daddy that taking Laramie in would be our gift to Baby Jesus this year."

The old man stopped twirling the matches and rubbed his hand across his scruffy beard. "Little one, it's okay to tell me whatever's on your mind. Your thoughts are safe with me, and I'll say to you I think that's a mighty worthy present to give to Baby Jesus."

"I hope so, because I'm not so sure we can get a real present to Him up in heaven."

"Well now, that's an interesting idea." His voice was real gentle, and I was beginning to think he was a nice man. I thought Daddy would understand this time about me talking to a stranger.

"What's your name, Mister?" I asked.

He didn't say straight out. It was like he had to remember his own name, and then he just said, "You can call me Mr. Josh. What may I call you?"

"My name's Katherine Joy Harding."

"Like your mama?"

"How do you know my mama's name?"

"Well, I just figured it was Mrs. Harding."

"Oh."

"So I should call you Katherine Joy Harding?"

"No, sir. Kate'll do. That's what my friends call me." I don't know why I said that, but it just felt all right to say it.

"Katherine Joy, you look a bit worried, child." He didn't call me Kate. "What put that serious look on your face?"

I didn't know why, but I told him that my mama had died and Laramie's mom had left, and that I didn't understand why such bad things had to happen. I hoped he couldn't tell I was about to cry.

"I'm sorry about your mama and your friend and your questions, but everything will be just fine, you'll see. Yes, little one, I think this story will have a happy ending."

Why would that old man say that about a story? That's what Pastor Simmons said. But how could this old man know the ending?

He was quiet for a few minutes, and I didn't make a sound. I just said, "Mm-hmm."

"Tell me about your mama. I just imagine she loved you a lot."

"Yes, sir. Mama made everything fun and special."

"She did, did she?"

"Yes, sir. Mama knew how to do everything, and she made even simple things special. She taught me a lot of things, mostly about making people happy. But then one day Mama got cancer. Daddy tried to make her better because taking care of folks is his job, and he wanted Mama to get well. And the doctors tried too, but they couldn't make her better, she was just too sick." I couldn't help it. The tears started coming. "We prayed God would heal her, and Granny Grace said He did because on September 28, Mama just quit holding my hand one night, and God came and got her and took her to heaven."

"He did, did He?"

"Yes, sir. He did." I didn't mean to and I didn't want to, but I just folded my arms over my face and leaned on my knees and cried. I cried hard like I hadn't cried in a long time. "I miss Mama. It's Christmas, and I miss my mama so much."

I felt his hand on my shoulder. "I know you miss your mama."

"It seems like forever she's been gone, and I don't want her to forget about me because she's so happy up in heaven."

"Oh, Kate. Your mama won't be forgetting one thing about you. Maybe she's happy in heaven because time is different there. Maybe to her, the time away from you doesn't seem so long."

He called me Kate. "But it seems pretty long to me." I wiped my eyes with my scarf.

"It hurts real bad sometimes to be separated from someone you love." He patted me on the back. "I want to tell you something, Kate. As you grow up, you'll be hearing your mama's voice in the things you say and in the things you teach your own children. And you'll see a little bit of her when you look into the mirror. Little one, your heart will always remember your mama."

We sat for a little while and didn't say anything. The sunlight coming through the window made his hair look like silver. Then he stood up, put the matchbook back in his pocket, and said out of the clear blue like he could read my mind, "Like I said, Kate, everything will be all right. You just remember to keep your faith. I can tell you have a real fine family, and your mama will love you forever."

Faith. Family. Forever. Now he sounded like Mama.

Then he reached underneath his coat and pulled out a magazine like he was going to read it, but he just laid it down on the table beside me. Right there on the front cover of the magazine was a picture. It was the prettiest redbird I ever saw, perched in a pine tree covered in snow.

Chapter Thirteen

I DON'T KNOW HOW long I stared at the picture on the magazine, but when I looked up, Mr. Josh was gone. I wiped my eyes with my scarf and looked around the room. I was alone. Where did he go?

I walked over to the door and nearly ran into Daddy coming in to get me. "Where'd he go?" I walked out into the hall and looked both ways. Mr. Josh wasn't there.

"Who are you talking about?" Daddy looked at me hard. "What's wrong, Kate?"

"Nothing. I was just talking to Mr. Josh about Mama and Laramie."

Daddy took me by the shoulders. "Who is Mr. Josh?"

"You didn't see him coming down the hall? He's an old man in a long overcoat."

"No, I didn't see anybody fitting that description." Daddy had that look on his face like the time he thought I had a fever. "Are you sure you're okay? You ready to go see Laramie?" Daddy took me by the hand and led me through the door.

I looked for Mr. Josh through every door we passed down the hall. He was just plain gone. Every room had people in it and flowers or balloons, but probably Laramie's wouldn't. "We shoulda brought some flowers or a teddy bear or something."

"You have a card. It'll be just fine." Daddy knocked lightly on the door and pushed it open.

Laramie was lying there with her head all bandaged up watching TV. I had my card in my coat pocket.

"Well, hello again, Laramie. Look who I brought to see you this afternoon?"

"Hi, Laramie. You sure do look a lot better than you did last night." Why did I have to say that? I'm sure that's just what she wanted to hear. "How are you today?"

"You girls visit a little bit. I need to make a call." Then Daddy stepped out.

I pulled the card out of my pocket and walked over to the edge of the bed. "I made you something, Laramie. I'm sorry I didn't have an envelope big enough."

Her eyes got big when she saw the two cardinals on a limb. She reached for the card. "Did you draw these?"

"Yep."

"You can really draw good, Kate. And you drew the birds, the kind like your mama told you to remember."

"Yep. I know how you like to feed the birds and all, and you're the only one in the class who lets me know when the redbird shows up at the bird feeder. So now you have some birds to remind you you're not alone. Maybe one of them can remind you of your mama."

"Thanks." She looked like she was going to cry and she didn't know what to say.

"Is it okay if I sit on your bed?"

"Sure." Laramie smoothed out the sheet, and I sat down.

"Everybody's been real worried about you."

She just shrugged, so I went on. "I'm glad you're okay and that you threw the rocks at my window, but I was wondering why you came to our house."

"I don't know. I guess I was scared, and I remembered what you said in class one day when you gave your report about what your daddy does. You said his job was to help people. So I just came to your house. I knew where you lived, just down the street from Emily and not far from the school."

"Yeah, Emily lives up the hill. But how did you know which room is mine?"

"That was the only light on upstairs, and I could see you sitting at your desk. And I wasn't throwing rocks; I found some acorns underneath the snow. I didn't want to break a window and be in more trouble than I was already in."

"Everybody's glad you came to our house. My daddy and my uncle Luke went out looking for you."

Laramie didn't say anything for a long time, and I just sat there on her bed. She was looking at the redbirds on the card. "Kate?"

"Uh huh."

"Last night when I came to your house, I sat under the tree a long time until all the lights went out, and there was a redbird."

"I think they roost in that tree in the nighttime because it's safe in the weather and it's close to where they feed."

"I was throwing acorns at your window. After that I don't remember very much."

I was glad the redbird made Laramie feel better.

"Kate, you think I'm in real big trouble?"

"I don't think so. I haven't heard my daddy say any-thing like that."

That's when Daddy walked in, and I was glad. I didn't want to talk about what Daddy said about Mr. Fields having a bad temper. Even if he wasn't the best father, he was still Laramie's daddy.

"Well, girls, you having fun?"

"Yes, sir," I said.

"Well good, because you're just getting started. Laramie, how would you like to come to our house for a few days? They're letting you out of here tomorrow morning."

"You mean to stay at your house? What about going home? Am I ever going home?" Laramie was holding that card I made her real tight.

"It's not a good idea for you to go home just yet. Your dad should be home in just a few days, and he thinks it's a good idea for you to stay with us. We have a doctor in the house, and you'll have Kate here to buddy around with. Doesn't that sound like a good idea?"

"I guess. I mean, yes, it does, sir. Thank you very much."

Laramie was using her good manners. Sometimes she does, and sometimes she doesn't.

"Then it's a deal." That was when Daddy handed me his notepad and pencil. "Now, I need to talk to someone, and while I'm gone, Kate, make a list of all of Laramie's favorite foods."

After Daddy left, Laramie asked me, "What's your favorite food, and your daddy's?"

I told her. She said those were her favorites too. I was glad because I didn't know who in the world would make it if she liked something weird. Daddy wasn't that great at cooking, and Aunt Susannah Hope wasn't up to it. Maybe Granny Grace would. But anyway we wouldn't have to worry about it now.

Daddy came back in to get me. "Laramie, you watch TV and rest this evening, and we'll be by to pick you up in the morning."

She was holding on to the card when Daddy and I walked out the door.

I went right upstairs when we got home. I didn't even say good-bye to Uncle Luke when he left to go shopping. I wasn't supposed to know about it so I couldn't tell him to buy the bloomin' ring anyway, like Daddy said. I cleaned up my room and put away some things I didn't want Laramie to see. I knew she was going to be my friend and all, but there were some things Mama gave me I wasn't ready to show her.

I cleaned out some drawers for her and boxed up my stuff and put it in the closet. I would ask Daddy to stop by the flower shop and get flowers for Laramie in the morning. He always did that for Mama. I'd make sure they were yellow, the happy color.

"Supper!" This time it was Daddy's voice, not Chesler's.

He was putting leftover chili in the bowls when I got downstairs, and the hot corn bread was on the table. "Pour the milk, will you, Kate?"

"Sure, Daddy. Don't you think we should have something green?"

"Green, you mean like grass?" Chesler was running around in circles in his sock feet like Grady chasing his tail.

"No, not like grass. I mean like green beans or a salad or some broccoli."

"We had yellow eggs this morning." Chesler was just trying to be cute. I ignored him.

"Mama's list on the bulletin board says we're supposed to eat something green every day."

"Okay, Kate, you can take your hands off your hips. You're right. I just wasn't thinking. Would a tossed salad do?"

"Yes, sir. I'll help you make it." Tossed salad to Daddy means only lettuce cut up in little pieces, so I got out the tomatoes and celery and cucumbers.

Last spoonful of chili, and I was at the sink washing dishes again. Daddy went to his office to pay bills, and Chesler went up to his room to play. I was thinking about Uncle Luke buying a diamond ring when the redbird showed up again in the cedar tree. The moon was reflecting so bright on the snow, it looked like a spotlight on that redbird. I couldn't help but think about the picture of the redbird on the magazine Mr. Josh had.

"You know, little redbird, maybe I'll just talk to you about what I know. Uncle Luke's thinking about getting married to Miss Applegate, and he might be buying her a ring right this very minute. Daddy wants him to, and I know I want him to. If my mama was here, she woulda just marched down to the jewelry store with Uncle Luke and picked one out. That's the good news, but I know some bad news too."

That redbird just fluttered her wings like she knew what was coming.

"My Aunt Susannah's sick. Daddy's afraid she's got what was wrong with Mama. When Mama got sick and told me she was going to heaven, I used to wish it was Aunt Susannah Hope. She didn't have any children to take care of, and I loved Mama so much. It just seemed better to me if my aunt had gone to heaven instead of Mama. Now I'm sorry I was thinking those things because I don't really want her to be sick. Uncle Don would be so sad, and poor Granny. One of her little girls has already left this earth without her, and Grandpa too. I hope I didn't make Aunt Susannah Hope be sick because I was thinking those things. I know I can tell you what I know, little bird, because you won't tell a soul. Oh, and I met Mr. Josh today."

I didn't hear Daddy come into the kitchen. "Who you talking to, Kate?"

"Just to myself. Daddy, I was just thinking I could put two smiley faces on my calendar tonight because we made Laramie happy two times. One for the card I made her and another for inviting her to come home with us."

"I think you're right, Kate. And if there's room, you can add a smiley face for me, because it made me so happy to see you welcome Laramie into our home."

"Thanks, Daddy." I liked that I made Daddy smile. "Guess tomorrow's the big day, so I'm going to my room to make sure everything's ready."

"Sure. Need any help?" Daddy put his arm around me and squeezed.

"No, sir, I think I can handle it."

"I'm sure you can. Turning in a bit early sounds good to me too. Now, how do we get Chesler to do the same?"

"That's not on my list. Besides you're the daddy, and that's your problem. My door's gonna be closed. So tell him that." I grinned at Daddy and walked out of the kitchen. I put one foot on the bottom stair and turned around. "And make sure Chesler brushes his teeth."

By the time I finished tidying up my room and putting everything away, it was late. Chesler's room was dark and quiet when I went down the hall to ask Daddy something. I headed back to my room when I saw there was no light coming from under Daddy's door. My question would have to wait till morning. Uncle Luke wasn't home, and I was the only one awake in the Harding house.

I put three smiley faces on my calendar, crawled into bed, and pulled the blanket up tight around my neck. All was quiet inside the house, but outside the wind was howling, and the naked branches of the elm tree rattled against the house. Now I might have been in bed and not making a sound, but I wasn't quiet on the inside. My brain was rattling like those tree limbs. I was really worried. Only a few more days until Christmas, and nobody had been able to answer my question about getting Mama's present to heaven. I wasn't sure if I'd ever figure it out, but I kept thinking.

I was just about to give up when it came to me. I sat straight up in bed like somebody had just turned the light on. Why hadn't I thought of it before? This was the best idea ever.

I lay back down. The wind had settled down, and my feather pillow felt so good. I thought my idea might work. It just had to.

CHAPTER FOURTEEN

THE SKY WAS gray, and God wasn't holding the snow back but letting it tumble. I was watching the flakes collect on the elm tree branches when Daddy came in my room.

"Little peep, rise and shine. It's snowing again. Looks like it'll be a white Christmas in Kentucky. Can't remember a December when we had so much snow."

"Guess we have a busy day today, Daddy?"

"Sure do. We have to get groceries and pick up Laramie, and Granny Grace is coming over to help with lunch."

I stretched long under the sheets. Mama always said I stretched like a cat and not to stretch any farther than I could walk back. "And will you add to your list putting some seeds in the bird feeder on my window? The birds will need it with the snow. And maybe you should have a talk with Chesler about Laramie coming to stay with us. He needs to use his manners and not be asking her any questions if he wants Santa Claus to make a stop here."

"Right again, little Miss Hands-on-Your-Hips. You make lists like your mama. What would I do without you? Anything else I should tell him?"

"You could tell him…never mind, he won't remember it anyway. I just don't want him bothering Laramie. Oh, and could we stop at the flower shop and get some daisies for Laramie?"

"Sure we can. That's a good idea." Daddy went to Chesler's room.

I put on nice school clothes since we were going back to the hospital. I walked by Uncle Luke's room on my way downstairs. His door was wide open, and I knew he was already in the kitchen with Daddy and Chesler. I thought maybe I would see a bag or a box from the jewelry store. If he bought a ring, he hid it, or maybe he already gave it to her. Sure enough I couldn't ask him.

I didn't stop at the bottom of the stairs to hear if they were talking grown-up stuff. I didn't want to know anything else that I had to keep to myself. Two secrets—that was enough. So I just walked straight on into the kitchen.

At breakfast Chesler asked Uncle Luke to take him ice skating down at the tennis courts by the school.

Daddy said, "Yeah, you'll have some fun. I saw the guys from the fire station hosing down the tennis courts yesterday. We don't get to do that every winter. Should be good skating this morning."

"Talked me into it, big brother. Let's do it, Chesler. I need to practice. I'm planning on taking Lisa skating later this week."

Ice skating? I guessed that was okay, but that was not what couples did on television when they were dating. "Why don't you dress up and take her dancing?"

Uncle Luke wiggled his eyebrows. "Skating or dancing? Dancing or skating?" He looked at Daddy. "Your daddy's the dancer. I think I'll have better luck on skates."

"Well, you better get her some flowers or perfume or something girly then."

"Why, yes, ma'am. I'll do just that." Uncle Luke got up from the table. "Get your skates, Chesler. We got some scooting around on the ice to do."

I was glad to be alone with Daddy without Chesler around. We did the grocery shopping and stopped to get the flowers. Granny Grace's good friend, Mrs. Rutherford, owned the flower shop across the street from the church. When we stepped through the door, Christmas music was playing, and whiffs of cinnamon and pine filled the air. Mrs. Rutherford came out from the back to greet us. She could have been Mrs. Santa Claus, wearing a bright red apron and a Santa hat on top of her wavy white hair. "Well, merry Christmas, you two. You're my first customers this chilly morning." She wiped her hands on her apron and shook Daddy's hand. "Haven't seen you in a while, John. What can I do for you this morning?"

"We need some flowers for one of Kate's friends who's in the hospital."

"Must be the little Fields girl. Heard about what happened to her. That's just a heaping ton of trouble that no little girl needs." Mrs. Rutherford headed toward the back. "Let me see what I have that just might put some color in that little girl's day."

I turned to Daddy. "I think Laramie would like yellow daisies, and they'd look real good in my room."

"Well that's certainly an idea you got, Kate, but look around. What would you think about red and white carnations? It is Christmas, remember."

Daddy was right. Today was not the day for yellow flowers. Christmas had arrived and set up camp at the Lilies of the Field flower shop. There was nothing in that flower shop that wasn't red, green, or white.

"That's fine." Maybe he thought daisies were only for Mama because they were her favorites.

We got to the hospital, and I carried in the Christmas carnations wrapped in green paper. Mrs. Rutherford had wrapped them up real pretty and tied them with red ribbon. We ran into Aunt Susannah Hope in the hospital lobby. She was leaving.

"Good morning, Susannah. What are you doing here?"

She pointed her finger at Daddy like he was in trouble. "Well, Luke stopped by the house yesterday and suggested I see my doctor and get some blood work done."

I knew all about blood work because they made Mama do that all the time.

"Are you here to see Laramie?" Aunt Susannah Hope asked.

"Yes, and to take her home with us. Since she's going to be around for Christmas, would you like to go up and meet her?"

I didn't think Aunt Susannah Hope would come with us, but she did. We were all quiet on the elevator up to the third floor. I think we were remembering the times Mama was here.

When we got to Laramie's room, Daddy let me go in first. I held the flowers behind my back so she couldn't see them. "Hey, Laramie. I hope you're feeling better this morning."

"I am. I'm feeling much better." Laramie was all dressed and sitting on the edge of her bed.

I pulled the flowers out. "Look, we brought you some flowers."

Her eyes got so big and her mouth opened like the choir teacher had told her to sing a high note. "Oh, flowers? Thank you. Thank you so much. They're really pretty."

The way she held onto those flowers with both hands and stared at them made me think nobody ever gave her flowers before.

Daddy walked over and put his hand on Laramie's shoulder and pointed toward my aunt. "Laramie, this is Kate's Aunt Susannah Hope. She wanted to come up and meet you. You'll see her again because she'll be at our house on Christmas Eve and again on Christmas Day."

Aunt Susannah Hope stepped closer to Laramie's bed. "Hi, Laramie. It's lovely to meet you, and we're so happy you'll be celebrating Christmas with us. I live up the hill from Kate."

Laramie stood up and used her best manners. "Thank you, ma'am. I think I know where you live. Don't you live in that pretty white house with the porch all around it and the fence with the morning glories and the roses in the summertime?"

"Yes, as a matter of fact, I do."

"My mom always liked that house and said she dreamed of living in one like it someday." Laramie looked back at her carnations.

"I think your mom and I would be great friends if she likes beautiful old houses and raised a little girl as sweet and pretty as you."

"Yes, ma'am, you'd like her."

I'm glad Aunt Susannah Hope said she would like Laramie's mom. Laramie probably thought nobody liked her mom since she just took off.

"Well, I'm so glad you're feeling better, and I'll see you again over at Kate's." Aunt Susannah patted Laramie's arm and left the room.

Laramie stepped across to the closet. "My things are in that sack, and I'm ready to go."

Daddy treated her like a young lady and took the sack. Laramie walked beside him like she was the prom queen, holding the card and flowers I gave her.

When we got home and walked in the front door, Laramie looked around like she had never seen anything like our house. "I don't remember any of this from the other night." But when we got to the den, she hesitated. "Oh, I think I remember this, the sofa, and that big stone fireplace. Yeah, I do remember. The fire was out, but the coals were still red." She turned around to me. "I didn't imagine all that, did I?"

"Nope, it was all here just like you remember, and Daddy put you on that sofa right there, and we covered you up in blankets. You just opened your eyes a few times and closed them again."

"Where's your little brother? What's his name?"

"That's Chesler. He's out ice skating with my uncle. And Chesler, oh you'll know it when he gets home. He's loud and annoying, and just don't ask him to sing, or you'll be sorry. Come on, I'll show you my room. I mean our room. You'll be staying with me."

Daddy had already put Laramie's things on my bed. "Okay, girls. Enjoy. Granny'll be here in a little while."

Laramie walked around looking at everything and asking more questions than Chesler. I had to explain about the calendar and the smiley faces and the bird feeder on the window. Then she saw the Books of My

Life on the shelf next to my desk. "What the heck are these? I mean, what are these?"

"Oh, those are the Books of My Life. My mama made one for every one of my birthdays. They have pictures and little stories about what I did that year. She made my birthday portrait with her wedding gown every year, even when I was a baby. When I was firstborn, she just laid me on the wedding gown to take the picture, and then when I got older, it was like playing dress up. Mama said my picture in her wedding gown every year was living proof I was growing up."

I pulled one off the shelf and opened it on my desk so she could see.

Laramie turned the pages slowly. "So what are you going to do now that your mama's not here?"

"I'm just planning to make my own books for myself, and I'll keep making them for Chesler too. One day he'll be glad I did."

She walked to the window. "And this is where the redbird comes to see you?"

"Mmm-hmm. There and in the cedar tree out back. I see her through the kitchen window when I wash dishes."

"That's so cool. I really love the card you made me. You can really draw." Then she walked over to my easel and the shelf where all my art stuff was. "This is the prettiest room I've ever seen. I know you miss your mama, but you're really lucky, Kate."

"Yeah, I guess. Mama let me choose the color for the walls, and then she painted the sunflowers and daisies."

"My mom painted my room too. We saw a room like it in a magazine, with blue walls and a blue ceiling. Mom left before she could paint the big fluffy clouds."

"How long's your mama been gone?"

"Three months, two weeks, and four days."

"You keep a count?"

"Every day. You don't?"

"Nope. I just know Mama went to heaven on September twenty-eighth." I would never forget that date. "You want to go back downstairs?"

"Whatever you want to do." Laramie was being so nice; she didn't seem like the tough girl I knew at school. Maybe she was just glad to be in a quiet place, away from all the troubles at home.

"Let's stay up here and listen to some music. They play Christmas music all day and all night on the radio. Daddy'll call us when it's time for lunch."

We were lying on the bed with the music turned up just talking when Emily came walking into my room with a white box in her hands. "Hi, Laramie. Hi, Kate. Your dad said I could come on up." She walked over to the bed and handed the box to Laramie. "Here, Laramie, these are for you. We got them at the bakery, and we got several kinds because we didn't know what was your favorite."

Laramie looked like she was scared to take the box. "Thanks." Laramie opened the box and pushed the lid back so we could see what was inside. There were oatmeal, chocolate chip, and green-iced cookies shaped like Christmas trees. "Here, Emily, you choose first."

Emily shook her head. "I shouldn't have one. It'll spoil my lunch."

Laramie still held the box out to Emily. "But I'd like it if you and Kate had one."

Emily acted all stiff and prickly. "No, I really shouldn't. I have to go. My mom's taking me to a special tearoom for lunch today. It's girls' day out."

I didn't know why Emily acted so…so uppity. I made a frowny face at her when she wasn't looking. Why'd Emily even bother to bring the cookies? She was just pretending to be nice. And how could she talk about her special time with her mom when she knew we didn't have our mamas?

I volunteered. "Here, I'll have a cookie." I picked out a frosted tree, and Laramie chose an oatmeal cookie.

While we munched on our cookies, Emily said to Laramie, "You had everybody in town worried about you, you know. My dad and Kate's dad and both her uncles were out in the cold looking for you."

Laramie put her cookie down.

I wanted to pull Emily's hair. Sometimes, she could be so…so right next to mean. Why would she think it wasn't okay for Laramie to swear but it was okay for her to be a brat?

I jumped in. "What Emily's trying to say is that so many people cared about you and were worried. We're just glad you're safe, and I'm really glad you're spending Christmas with us."

Emily got bug-eyed. "Oh. She's staying here for the holidays?"

"Yes, Laramie's here for several days, so I'm not sure when we'll be seeing you."

"Fine. Did you figure out how to get your mama's Christmas present to heaven yet?"

I knew Emily wasn't asking that like she wanted an answer. She was just being bratty again, and I wanted to ring her neck. "Yeah, I think I have."

"So, tell me."

"No, not yet."

I was glad to hear Mrs. Peterson calling Emily from the bottom of the stairs. "Come on, Emily. We have things to do."

Emily turned around prissy-like with her proper ponytail swinging. "Bye. I'll call you later, Kate."

Somebody taught Laramie well because even after Emily was so snippety, Laramie still said, "Thank you very much for the cookies, Emily. That was really sweet of you."

I wanted to slam the door when Emily walked out, but I didn't. "I'm sorry about Emily. She isn't always so..." I couldn't even think of a word to say. I just squinted my eyes and shook my head. "Maybe if she didn't wear that ponytail so tight her nose wouldn't be stuck up in the air so high."

"That's okay. Emily's your friend, but I know she doesn't like me."

I mocked Emily in her whiny voice. "My mom's taking me to a special tearoom for lunch today. It's girls' day out." I looked back at Laramie. "What kind of friend says that when she knows my mama's in heaven and your mom is gone?"

"Eat your cookie, Kate. Emily's just a snotty-nosed brat, and if I felt like it..." Laramie stopped talking for a second, then she said, "But she was really nice to bring the cookies."

I knew Laramie was working at using her manners. "Emily just doesn't like your swearing and stuff," I explained. "But she just doesn't understand the swearing's not who you are 'cause you can be really nice."

"Okay, then I'll try to watch my mouth," Laramie said matter-of-factly. "My mom didn't let me swear, but my dad swears and he never says anything about me swearing. But I won't swear at your house."

"That's good, 'cause swearing would make Aunt Susannah Hope break out in hives, and Granny just might do something with a washrag and soap that you'd remember for a long time." I laughed a little when I said that.

Laramie brushed the cookie crumbs off the comforter into her hand and threw them in the wastebasket. "Okay, I got it, Kate. I'll do like Mom taught me."

After that we just listened to music and ate cookies and talked until I heard Uncle Luke and Chesler come in. I switched off the radio. "Let's go downstairs. It's getting close to lunchtime."

Daddy was putting food on the table. Granny turned around from the stove. "Well, hello, Laramie, I'm Kate's granny. You can just call me Granny Grace. Everybody else does."

"Yes, ma'am. Kate told me about how you live on a farm. We used to visit my grandma when she lived on a farm."

Uncle Luke came down the stairs with my brother over his shoulder and a tube of ointment in his hand. He put Chesler down and opened the tube. "It won't hurt nearly as bad as scraping your chin did when you fell on the ice."

Granny Grace always said that Chesler was just an accident waiting to happen. And wouldn't you know it, the only place on Chesler's body not covered by three layers of wool was where he got hurt skating? Uncle Luke finished his doctor's routine, and I tugged on his shirt. "Uncle Luke, this is Laramie. And Laramie? This is my uncle Luke and my little brother, Chesler."

"Very pleased to meet you, Laramie. I'd shake your hand, but I don't think you'd like this slimy medicine." Uncle Luke headed for the sink to wash his hands.

Chesler just stood there like he'd never seen a girl before, and Uncle Luke walked over and patted her on the shoulder. Then he asked, "Hey, Laramie, would you do me a favor?"

She looked real surprised. "Sure. I'll try."

"Sit down here. I need to practice my doctoring. Would you allow me to look at your stitches?"

"If you want to."

He pulled out a chair from the table for her, and he was careful removing the bandages. "Hey man, this is beautiful. Whoever stitched you up must have taken embroidery lessons from Granny Grace. Anybody want to see?"

"Not me." I backed away a little.

But Chesler had to poke his nose in. "I do, I do. I never saw stitches before. Not in somebody's face."

I pinched him so he wouldn't say something dumb. But it didn't do any good.

"Your face looks like Kate's rag doll." I pinched him again but he barely flinched.

Granny kept busy, but Daddy took a look. "Healing nicely, and the swelling's gone down."

Laramie just sat there real still and quiet. I think our family was a big change for her, but everybody fussed over her like she was a princess just arrived from some place special. I was glad.

"Okay, let's eat. Everybody grab a chair, and Laramie, you sit over there next to Kate, and Chesler, you sit on the other side of Laramie." Granny Grace was directing traffic again.

Chesler stood in his tracks. "But she's a...she's a..."

"She's a what, Chesler?" Uncle Luke was pinching Chesler's ear.

"Uh...a girl."

"Yeah, and a pretty one. Just practice. One of these days you'll like sitting by a pretty girl."

"You like to sit by Miss Applegate?"

"Yeah, I do. Sit down, before I pinch both of your ears."

I never was happier to see a big dish of Granny's home-made-from-scratch, three-cheese macaroni. Laramie looked just as happy as me, because she took two big helpings.

After lunch I didn't have to help with the dishes. The rest of the day we just did things in my room. Talking and listening. That was how you learned about some-body. You asked a lot of questions, and you listened to what they said. Sometimes Laramie would use a bad word, and then she'd stop like someone told her it was a bad word, and then she'd say something nice again. She told me about the night she ran away.

"Were you scared in that shed at school?"

"Sorta. It was really cold and dark in there, but I fig-ured I was better off in that shed than I was if I went back home, at least for a while. I was really glad when it got daylight, but I still didn't come out of the shed. My head was hurting, and I kept going back to sleep. And when I wasn't sleeping, I was thinking."

"What were you thinking about?"

"I was thinking about what to do. I didn't have any money, so I couldn't go to my aunt's on the bus. She lives a long ways away. I thought about breaking into the motorcycle shop to get some money, but I was afraid my dad would be there. I didn't know anybody else knew I was gone, let alone that the whole town was looking for me."

Then she got real quiet and got that look in her eyes like Mama used to get sometimes when her mind went somewhere else and she didn't want to talk anymore.

I waited for a little while, and then I asked her if she wanted to do an art project. She liked that idea. And when we got tired of that, we fixed each other's hair. I was careful with hers because of her stitches and stuff. I liked having her around.

Daddy let us stay up late, and I gave Laramie one of my gowns to sleep in. And I gave her a pair of socks to keep her feet warm. It had stopped snowing, and when I turned out the light, the moon was shining bright through the window. Laramie was curled up like a cat on the far side of my double bed, but I knew she wasn't asleep.

I got into bed, and for a little while we both just lay there, breathing. When the dark was warm and quiet, I said, "When do you miss your mama the most?"

Laramie rolled over on her back. "I don't know. I just miss her all the time. What about you?"

"I think I miss Mama mostly at bedtime. We just had these things we did every night, prayers and smiley faces and talking about the day. I miss that, and I miss knowing she's just down the hall."

"Yeah, me too. Daddy told me yesterday that she's okay and he hoped she was coming home, but I don't know." Laramie paused. "Can I tell you a secret, Kate?"

"Sure. I won't tell a soul." I turned over on my back too and just watched the shadows of the tree limbs on the ceiling.

"Before she went away, I think Mom came into my room one night and told me she was going away for a little while, but she'd be back."

"For real?"

"Yeah, for real, I think. But I don't know for sure. Sometimes I think it really happened, but sometimes I think I was just dreaming or wishing it so."

"I hope it's for real." I got quiet for a minute. "Can I tell you a secret too?"

"You want to tell me a secret? Nobody in our class ever told me a secret."

"Yeah, this is a big secret. I made my mama a Christmas present."

"That's your secret, but Emily knows?"

"Well, Emily sort of knows. I mean, she knows about the present and all, but she doesn't know my real, real secret. I've been trying to figure out how to get Mama's present to heaven. I asked Pastor Simmons and Uncle Luke and Miss Applegate, and nobody knows, but I finally figured it out." I told Laramie what I figured out and what I was planning to do.

She promised not to tell anyone. I knew she wouldn't. I wanted to tell her my other two secrets, about Uncle Luke asking Miss Applegate to marry him and about my Aunt Susannah Hope being sick, but I figured one secret on the first night was enough.

We stopped talking, and the room was real quiet for a little while. "Good night, Laramie."

"G'night, Kate." Then she rolled over facing the wall. "Kate?"

"Uh-huh."

"You think the redbird's in the cedar tree?"

"I don't know because it's been snowing, but I know she's out there somewhere. I just hope she's warm."

Chapter Fifteen

*D*ADDY HAD TO work all day Thursday, so Granny Grace came over to stay with us. Laramie had been with us only a day, but I already knew I liked having her around. With Mama gone and all, I didn't have a woman around much, except when my aunt or granny visited. But Laramie was my age, and she liked the things I liked, and I was teaching her how to draw. I asked Daddy if I could get a sketchbook and pencils for Laramie for Christmas. I even told Daddy I wanted to pay for it with my own saved-up allowance.

Thursday night after supper Miss Lisa came over, and Uncle Don and Aunt Susannah Hope and Granny Grace joined us too. We all bundled up and headed for church to do some Christmas caroling. Miss Applegate had brought red Santa hats for everybody to wear, including Laramie.

Pastor Simmons met us at the door. "Well looka here. We have the whole O'Donnell and Harding clan. And here's Miss Laramie. Now don't you look like a cheerful bunch?"

Granny Grace stepped right up. "That's right, we're here to spread the cheer!"

About that time I saw a real pretty lady walk up next to the pastor. She was kind of tall, slim, and tan, and she had blonde hair like Miss Lisa's. I didn't remember seeing her before.

Pastor Simmons took the cup of coffee from her. "You may remember my sister, Evie. She visits from time to time. Sis, these are some of my favorite folks." Then he introduced everyone by name, and she shook everybody's hand.

Aunt Susannah Hope was last. "It's good to see you again, Evie. Are you here to spend the holidays with your brother?"

"Thank you. And yes, I'm here for Christmas. Last year convinced me there was no more beautiful place to spend Christmas than in Cedar Falls. Not much snow where I live." She smiled; she could have starred in a tooth paste commercial.

Granny Grace chimed in. "And where is that?"

"Right now, I'm living in South Florida."

"Yes, my sister, the artist gypsy bird. I call her that because she mostly lights places. I'm not sure she lives anywhere. I'm working on her to light here for a spell."

I couldn't hold it any longer. "You're an artist?"

"Yes. I'm a photojournalist, and I paint a little."

"What is a photojournalist?"

"I travel around the world taking pictures and writing stories about what I see. And I hope that what I see and capture in my photographs might cause some people to look at the world differently."

The pastor looked down at her. "Yes, I keep telling her she could fly right back to Cedar Falls after her travels and open her studio right here. I think I'm making a little headway."

I never met anybody like Evie before. "Did you take the pictures in the pastor's office? Where do you go and what do you see? Could I see some of your pictures? And do you have lots of cameras?"

She put her pointing finger square in the middle of my forehead. "And you, my new little friend, you have a very inquisitive mind. Let's see. Yes, I took the pictures in Fletcher's office, and yes, I do have lots of cameras. I travel mostly to Central and South America, and I see far more than I have time to tell you about right now. So maybe I can show you what I see in my photographs. We can talk about that later."

Before anybody could say anything else, I said it. It just popped right out of my mouth like Chesler used to squirt out his pacifier. "That's what I want to be when I grow up—an artist and a photographer." I never even thought about it before because I didn't know I could be one.

"Fantastic. It's a great life doing what you love and capturing images that stir people to think." Miss Evie smiled at me.

Things were really getting interesting when Mrs. Crouch, she's our organist, stopped everything. She divided us into caroling groups. Our whole family and the Hancocks were supposed to go to the Cedar Falls Care Home and walk up and down the halls singing Christmas carols. Mrs. Crouch gave us battery-operated candles to carry while we sang. That was good because if the candles were real, Chesler would probably set something on fire.

I saw the artist standing next to Pastor Simmons. "Daddy, can we ask the pastor's sister to go with us?" "Well, don't you think she might want to go with her brother and his family? She really doesn't know us."

"Yeah, but we could ask her. She could get to know us."

Daddy shook his head. "We just met her. Maybe another time."

"But there might not be another time."

"You can see her when we all come back to the church after the caroling."

"Okay. But Daddy, she knows all about cameras."

"And she'll still know all about them when we see her again."

We all loaded up in our car and left for the care home. Chesler appointed himself our song leader, and he sang louder than everybody as we walked up and down the halls. Lots of old people came to the doors dressed in their pajamas. I was glad Chesler was singing because he would have said something embarrassing otherwise. Laramie and I just looked at each other and smiled.

When we had sung all the Christmas carols we knew, we loaded up and headed out again. Our next stop was Mr. Pruitt's house. He was real old, older than Granny, and he lived alone. His lights were on, but he didn't have decorations for Christmas. We huddled together on his sidewalk and sang "Silent Night."

We were singing "The First Noel" when Mr. Pruitt came to the door, tall and so skinny he had to wear suspenders to keep his pants up. He invited us all in and offered to make coffee, but Daddy told him we had another place to stop. I didn't think fourteen people would have fit in his house anyway.

Before we left, Granny handed Mr. Pruitt a box of her famous Japanese fruitcake. When he opened the lid, I thought his broomstick legs were gonna give out. Mr. Pruitt was so glad about our singing and about that cake that tears leaked from his eyes.

The next stop was Mrs. Funderburke's. She lived down the street from Laramie's house. Laramie's eyes were glued to the car window when we rode down Potters Way. No lights on, not even Christmas lights at her house. I didn't know what she was thinking, but I was sad for her. Maybe I could get her to think about something else like Granny tried to do with me when she thought I was sad. So I tapped her arm and whispered, "Did you see that old trunk on Mr. Pruitt's porch?"

She still looked out the window. "Yeah."

"I wonder what was in it. I'll bet it's old and important and maybe has something valuable in it, like a treasure or some old letters or antique jewelry."

"Yeah."

"Maybe we could take him some cookies one day and ask him."

She shrugged. My plan didn't work, and I was glad to get to Mrs. Funderburke's and start our let's-make-somebody-happy Christmas caroling again. Maybe Laramie would forget about her lonely house.

Mrs. Funderburke came to the door when we first started singing. She had on a bright red housecoat and her hair was in curlers. Mama would have said Mrs. Funderburke was just fluffy. For sure, she didn't need suspenders like Mr. Pruitt.

We finished singing, and she thanked us for coming. Then Chesler said out loud, loud enough the firemen could have heard him down at the fire station, "Aren't you going to give a fruitcake to Mrs. Funderburke?"

I was standing next to him and reached around and covered his mouth with my hand. He yelped because I touched the injury on his chin. After Chesler got quiet, everybody turned and looked at Granny Grace. She looked like she coulda pulled Chesler's tongue out and used it to sharpen Grandpa's old straight-edge razor. "Well, I seem to be all out of cakes tonight, Mrs. Funderburke, but I'll make a fresh one just for you and bring it by tomorrow."

Granny had enough bricks for her heavenly mansion, and for sure, Mrs. Funderburke hadn't missed eating too many slices of cake. But if I knew Granny, Mrs. Funderburke would have a slice of Cedar Falls's finest Japanese fruitcake for her dessert tomorrow at lunch.

After we left Mrs. Funderburke's, we went back to the church for hot chocolate and donuts. I told Laramie to save us a seat on the piano bench and I'd bring her some hot chocolate.

Just when I sat down, Pastor Simmons came over with his son, whose hair stood up in wild cowlicks from wearing a stocking cap. "Harry, tell Kate what we read last night."

Harry hung onto his daddy's leg and wiggled around it like Chesler used to do. "Daddy was readin' to me about Charlotte the spider and Wilbur the pig."

"He did? That's one of my favorites. How do you like it?"

"We like it."

"Good, if you like that one, then maybe your daddy will read you the one about the cricket in Times Square next." I just had to touch that hair, so I patted him on the head.

Harry looked up at his daddy. "We can read that one, Daddy?"

"Yes, Harry, we can read it next. And we have Kate to thank for reminding me of these good books." Mrs. White called the pastor over, and he took Harry's hand to walk off. Then Pastor Simmons turned around. "Kate, sorry I didn't have an answer for you last week. I hope you're okay about all that." He looked at me over his little round glasses and stretched his eyes like he was protecting our secret.

"Yes, sir, you helped me. It's okay now." I wasn't about to tell him I had figured it out.

After he left, Laramie slid closer to me on the piano bench. "Does he know your secret?"

"No. I went to his office to ask him, but he didn't know. So we just talked about stories and books."

"But you figured it out, so aren't you going to tell him?"

"Not on your life. If he knew what I'm planning, he'd just tell Daddy. And there goes my plan. I gotta see if it works first, then I'll tell him."

I saw Daddy and Miss Evie over in the corner talking. Daddy was smiling a little. I hoped they could be friends. Then I'd know two artists, Miss Lisa and Miss Evie, and maybe I'd get to see all her cameras and her photographs.

When we got home, Daddy said it was Laramie's night to take the peppermint candy off the Advent calendar. Then he had to explain about the Advent calendar and how Mama made it when I was little because I nearly made her crazy asking how many days 'til Christmas. "Okay, just a few more peppermints left! When you wake up Sunday morning, it'll be Christmas Day."

"My new skates'll be under the tree when I wake up Sunday," Chesler announced. "Uncle Luke, then we can go skating again and my feet won't hurt and make me fall."

If Chesler didn't get those skates, I didn't want to be here for that scene.

"You got it, red top. Lisa and I are going skating tomorrow night if she thinks she can keep up with me." Uncle Luke brushed Miss Lisa's nose with his finger.

"Okay, everyone under the age of twenty-one, it's bedtime." Daddy smiled at Uncle Luke. "Chesler, brush your teeth. Brush them twice. The first time because you ate a donut and the second time for opening your mouth, and now Granny's got to bake another cake tomorrow."

"Yes, sir."

Uncle Luke put his arm around Miss Lisa. "I think this pretty lady and I'll take a walk down the street to see the Christmas lights. Good night, Laramie, and you bunch of Hardings."

We gave good-night hugs and took off up the stairs. I heard Daddy say, "Enjoy your walk. I'll have a fire for you when you get back."

Chesler kept the water running for a long time. That didn't mean he brushed his teeth. But he turned off the water and came flying outta there when I told him it was Laramie's turn in the bathroom.

A few minutes later Laramie and I crawled into bed and pulled up the covers. I liked having someone to talk to when we turned the lights out. It didn't seem as lonesome. "People in love do crazy things, don't you think?" I asked.

"You mean like your uncle Luke and Miss Applegate?"

"Yeah, why else would they walk in the snow when it's twelve degrees to see Christmas lights we just drove by?" I paused. "Can you keep another secret?"

"Yeah, nobody can squeeze secrets outta me."

"Good. I think Uncle Luke's going to ask Miss Lisa to marry him."

"He is? When?"

"I hope it's while he's home for Christmas."

"Did he say it?"

"Not exactly. I heard him and my daddy talking, and Daddy thought he should ask her. But I'm not supposed to know any of this. It was grown-up talk, and they didn't know I was listening."

"Yeah, what is it with adults? Do they think we don't have ears until we get old? I heard a police officer talking to the doctor the other day about my dad being in jail."

"Is he going to be in jail long?"

Laramie jerked the covers. "I don't really know for sure. My dad didn't explain it to me when he visited me at the hospital."

I heard her sniffle and wondered if I should get her a tissue. "Are you okay, Laramie?"

But she wasn't, because just then Laramie started sobbing. I mean shoulder-shaking sobbing out loud.

I was scared and didn't know what to do, so I went out in the hall and called Daddy. He came right up those stairs just like he used to when Mama called him.

"What's wrong, Laramie?" Daddy sat down on the bed next to Laramie. I stood right behind him.

She was crying like she hadn't ever cried before, like all the hurt she stored up had come tumbling out. "It's all my fault my dad's in jail," she sobbed.

"Laramie, whoa, now wait a minute. It's not your fault your dad's in jail, and I don't think he'll be there long. He just made some bad choices, and now he's dealing with the consequences."

"But if I hadn't run away, then nobody would know, and Dad would still be at home."

Daddy smoothed Laramie's hair out of her face and handed her another tissue. "It's okay to cry, Laramie. Just cry it all out. But when that's done, let me tell you what's going to happen to you. You're going to stay right here with us until you can go home."

Laramie just kept crying. "But I really want to see my mom and my dad."

"I know you do, Laramie." Then Daddy put his arm around me. "Kate and I know you want to see them. We know about wanting to see somebody real bad. But I tell you what, I promise I'll make some calls in the morning. And we'll see what we can find out about when you'll see your parents. How's that?"

She finally stopped crying. "Thank you, Mr. Harding. Thank you so much."

"You're welcome, Laramie. Now you two can just lie here and talk for a little while, and then you need to get some sleep. Okay?"

Daddy hugged me, and I crawled into bed next to Laramie. He turned out the lights and closed the door. Now I knew how Daddy felt when me or Chesler started crying about missing Mama. I didn't like it when Laramie cried and I couldn't do a thing to make her quit. I just stayed quiet, and she sniffled like Chesler did when he tried to stop crying.

My room was so bright it looked like a light was on. It had to be the full moon shining on the snow. I knew there'd be about a gazillion stars in the sky. I whispered, "Laramie, you asleep?" I got out of bed and went to the window.

"No," she whispered back.

"Get up. Come over here."

Laramie got up and stood beside me.

"Look at all the stars out tonight! Let's make a wish before we go to sleep."

"Okay." She was still sniffling a little bit.

"I know what I'm wishing for, but if I tell, it won't come true." I wished my plan was going to work and I wouldn't get in trouble. And I wished Laramie would have a smile on her face tomorrow and Uncle Luke would ask Miss Lisa to marry him.

"I know what I'm wishing for too."

"Okay. Hold my hand and find one star, then close your eyes and start wishing on it." When I got through wishing and opened my eyes and looked out, Uncle Luke and Miss Applegate were standing on the side-walk, kissing just like it wasn't cold, and they didn't care who saw them. It was like the whole big moon was just shining on them.

Laramie and I looked at each other, then she said, "I hope Miss Applegate's wishing on a star."

After wishing, we climbed back in bed. My pillow might as well have been a cloud because my head was still in the stars. Laramie was quiet, and I didn't even remember going to sleep.

CHAPTER SIXTEEN

*F*RIDAY MORNING DADDY went to work and Granny stayed at the farm to make Mrs. Funderburke's cake. Uncle Luke was keeping us all day.

We had a snowball fight out back by the creek. He said it wasn't safe for Laramie to do that with her stitches and all, so he gave her a pad and pencil and told her to keep score. I think she missed some points because she kept looking at the redbird in the cedar tree.

When Uncle Luke got cold and tired, we went in and warmed by the fire. He said we could make snow cream because the snow was fresh. He made it with lots of sugar and vanilla, and it tasted so good.

Any other time, Uncle Luke woulda played games with us all day, but he was acting fidgety. He'd start a game, and then he'd say, "I need to do something. Go ahead and finish without me. I was going to win anyway." Then he'd disappear upstairs for a while before coming back down to check on us.

As soon as Daddy got home at the end of the day, Uncle Luke went upstairs and stayed. We were still at the table finishing supper when he came into the kitchen. He had on his best sweater, and his hair was combed real good, and he smelled like Daddy did for church. He said, "I'm leaving," and went to the closet, grabbed his coat and skates, and slammed out the door.

We just sat there all surprised like because it happened so fast. Before we said a word, he stuck his head back in the door and said, "Wish me luck. And Chesler, plug in the tree lights. Don't you know it's Christmas?" He slammed the door again.

Daddy said, "Chesler, do what your uncle said. Then go get your bath and put on your pj's. When that's all done, come back downstairs. We're playing Skip-Bo tonight. You and me against the girls, what do you say to that?"

"We're gonna wi-in. We're gonna wi-in," Chesler sang as he left the kitchen.

Daddy didn't get up from the table. He had a big smile on his face. "Laramie, I told you last night, I'd make some calls today, and I did. I went down to the jail on my lunch break to see your dad. Sweetie, your dad is so sorry about all of this. He wanted me to tell you how much he loves you and how sorry he is for everything."

Laramie didn't move a muscle. She didn't cry or smile or anything. "Is he coming home?"

"Well, he's working on it, but it's going to take a few days. The police know that the drugs were not his because one of the guys confessed. But until they get this straightened out, you'll stay here. Before they let him out, they need to make sure he gets help to take better care of you and himself."

"And he'll take better care of my mom if she comes home?"

"I know he wants to. Your dad's a hardworking man, and I think this episode was a wake-up call for him. It really scared him when you ran away. Anyway, you have a place right here, and I tell you, I think things are going to be just fine. I wouldn't say that if I didn't believe it to be true."

I chimed in. "Daddy's telling you the truth, Laramie. He never lied and told me when Mama was sick that she would get better. He always told me the truth. He just said she would be better when she got to heaven."

"Thank you, Mr. Harding. And thank you for going out in the cold to look for me. I know everybody probably hates me because of what I did."

"No, no. That's not true. You did the best thing you knew to do in getting out when you did. We're just sorry you felt you had nowhere to go. But that's all in the past. You're safe now, and things are going to be so much better." Daddy came around the table and hugged us both. "You two girls are getting to be such good friends. I'm so glad."

We had just finished cleaning the kitchen when Chesler came in wearing mismatched superhero pajamas. "Chesler! Just look at yourself. You have on Spiderman bottoms and a Superman top."

"I don't care 'cause I'm Superspiderman." He flexed his muscles.

"Superspiderman?" Laramie asked. She looked at me, I looked at her, and we both just burst out laughing. "Chesler, you're just what we need around here—Superspiderman." She smiled real big.

Daddy came in with the cards. "Well, Superspiderman, let's see how well you play Skip-Bo."

That wishing on a star must work. One of my wishes just came true. Laramie smiled—first time today.

We started the game, and Daddy and Chesler pulled ahead. Laramie hadn't played Skip-Bo before, so it took a little while for her to catch on. The phone kept ringing while we played, and Daddy got up and talked on the phone in his office by the garage. Every time it rang, I expected him to come back and say, "Okay, gotta go to work, so get your things. Aunt Susannah Hope's going to watch you while I'm gone." But every time he came back, he just started playing again and didn't say a word.

We were on our third game when Uncle Luke and Miss Lisa came home. That was a surprise. They were supposed to be out on a date.

They came straight into the kitchen and Uncle Luke got out the milk and started making hot chocolate for everybody. We just kept playing cards while he and Miss Lisa giggled and got out cups and stirred the mix and threw on the marshmallows. They gave everybody a mug, and they stood at the end of the table. Uncle Luke looked at Chesler. "Don't even think about it, buddy. Don't you take one sip of that hot chocolate. We need to make a toast."

Daddy smiled bigger than he'd smiled in a long time, just like Uncle Luke was smiling.

Then Uncle Luke raised his mug and said, "Kate and Chesler, I want to introduce you to your new aunt-to-be. This is for her. Cheers." He clicked his mug against Miss Lisa's and kissed her on the cheek.

I squealed. "You're getting married? For real?"

Before Uncle Luke could finish saying, "Come June, you'll have another aunt," we were on our feet doing a group hug, and nobody spilled hot chocolate, not even Chesler.

Then Uncle Luke said, "Lisa, why don't you tell them how I proposed?"

Miss Lisa giggled a little before she started telling us. "Well, Luke took me to the small pond at your Granny's house to go ice skating. It was really very beautiful. The moonlight on the pond made it look like the ice was glowing from underneath. It was too cold for his cassette player to work, so he started singing while we skated." She looked at Uncle Luke and smiled.

"Go on, tell them the rest."

"Well, I didn't know what his plans were, and I think I might have spoiled them when I fell down really hard, flat on my back. So he knelt down beside me and made sure I was all right, and then he said, 'If you'll marry me, I'll help you up.' Then he pulled this out of his pocket."

Miss Lisa stuck her hand out, and there was the ring. I knew he had it somewhere. It looked like he had chiseled a chunk of pure ice out of the pond and stuck it on her finger.

Daddy kissed Miss Applegate-soon-to-be-Aunt-Lisa on her cheek. "I'm just glad the pond was frozen enough for you two to skate on. I don't know that you could count on me to rescue you in that cold water." Then Daddy gave Uncle Luke a bear hug. "Just couldn't wait until Christmas, could you, little brother?"

"Nope. My big brother told me not to waste another day."

We stayed up talking a while. Daddy just about cried when Uncle Luke asked him to be his best man. I thought Miss Lisa musta been thinking about all this a long time 'cause she asked me to be a junior bridesmaid, and she wanted Chesler to be the ring bearer. I hoped she knew what she was getting into with Chesler.

I knew I was running out of time to tell Chesler my plan for getting Mama's Christmas present to her in heaven. Tonight had to be the night. "It's bedtime, Daddy. I'll take Chesler up, and Laramie and I'll turn in too. You can stay up and talk about things with Uncle Luke and Miss Lisa."

"Thanks, Kate. That's sweet of you."

I hugged Uncle Luke and Miss Lisa, and Laramie did too. Chesler crawled all over Uncle Luke and then he climbed in Miss Lisa's lap and hugged her like he used to hug Mama. I thought I saw a tear in her eye.

Daddy followed us to the bottom of the stairs and hugged Laramie and then kissed me good night. He high-fived Chesler and said, "Now, you do what your sister tells you to, little buddy, you hear me?"

"Yes, sir." Then all the way up the stairs, he sang that song about Santa Claus coming to town.

Laramie started laughing at him again. She thought he was funny 'cause she didn't know how annoying he could be sometimes. When we got to the top of the stairs, Laramie headed to my room.

I grabbed the sleeve of her sweater. I whispered, "Come on, we're going to Chesler's room."

She got that what-for look on her face, but she followed me anyway and didn't ask any questions. We went into Chesler's room and closed the door.

Chesler turned around. "Wait, I gotta brush my teeth, and why is Laramie in here?" Tonight of all nights, he wanted to brush his teeth.

"Look, Chesler, I won't make you brush your teeth tonight if you'll just crawl into bed and be quiet. I have to tell you something."

"Okaayy!" He made a beeline for his bed. "But what about Laramie?"

I helped him turn down the covers, and he crawled in bed. "Laramie's in here 'cause she's part of what I need to tell you. But Chesler, you can't tell anybody. Do you understand?"

"It's a secret?"

"Yeah, a big secret, and if you tell anybody, I mean anybody, then Mama won't get her present for Christmas, and we'll all be so sad. And besides, I'll be so mad with you till…" I shook my head. "You just have to keep this secret, and I mean it."

For once in his whole life Chesler listened, and he didn't ask a bunch of numbskull questions. I told him my whole plan, how Laramie was going to help me, and then I told him about the one thing I needed him to do besides keeping the secret.

He sat up in the bed. "Oh, Kate, this is like an adventure. I want to do what you and Laramie are doing."

"You can't, Chesler. This is my plan, and I'm sticking to it. It's too late to make any changes. But promise me, I mean really promise me, you won't tell anybody, not Daddy, not Uncle Luke, not Granny, nobody, okay?"

"I really, really, really promise, Kate. I won't tell nobody."

I kissed him on top of his head and turned on the night-light next to his bed. "Good night, Chesler."

He crawled under the covers. "Good night, Kate, and good night, Laramie." He blew Laramie a kiss.

Laramie went over and kissed him on his cheek. "Good night, Superspiderman."

We tiptoed down the hall to my room, talked over my plan one more time, and got ready for bed. Laramie put her clothes away while I put one smiley face on my calendar. "Want to look at the stars again tonight?"

She put on the pair of slippers I lent her and headed straight for the window. "Yeah. Let's see if it's still snowing."

I turned out the light and walked to the window. The moon was so bright, and the elm tree branches made shadows on the snow. We stood there together watching the snow fall, but we didn't say a word. I didn't know what Laramie was thinking, but I was thinking Friday had been a happy day.

Two of my wishes had come true. I wanted Laramie to smile, and she did. She even laughed at Chesler two times. And I wished Uncle Luke would ask Miss Lisa to marry him, and he did. I even got something I didn't wish for. I was going to be a junior bridesmaid!

My plans for getting Mama's Christmas present to heaven were made. Laramie was going to help, and I had told Chesler my plan. I looked at the sky and all those stars twinkling, and I wondered where Mama was, but this time instead of wishing, I prayed that my plan would work out. Because only God could make sure that Mama got her present in heaven.

CHAPTER SEVENTEEN

*D*ADDY WAS WHISTLING this morning. I hadn't heard him whistle in a long time. Mama used to like it when he whistled. She'd say, "Listen, Kate, your daddy's whistling. That's a beautiful sound coming from a happy heart. He's out in the garage, and I'll bet he's building something we're going to like." She liked his harmonica playing too. Sometimes he and Mama would sit in the front porch swing, and he would play until she fell asleep.

One night I heard them on the porch talking about what was going to happen after she went to heaven. Daddy told her that she was the glue that held the family together. But Mama said it wasn't glue that held this family together. She said it was love, and it was going to take more love and more patience and more of everything when she was gone. Then things got quiet, and he played his harmonica for a long time. When Mama went to heaven, he quit playing. I think it was because all he knew how to play were sad, slow songs, and he didn't want to be sadder than he already was.

Hearing him whistle this morning made me feel like I did when I saw that redbird in the cedar tree out back or when Grandpa would get out his fiddle and play a jig. Maybe Daddy was whistling because Uncle Luke and Lisa were getting married, or maybe

Christmas Eve made him whistle. I didn't care. I just liked hearing it.

Laramie was still sleeping. I just lay quiet and let her sleep. Uncle Luke said rest was the best thing for her. The first two nights, she moved around all night, pulling on the covers and turning and twisting and whimpering. But last night she slept quiet-like. I thought when Daddy told her it wasn't her fault her dad went to jail and that he would be out soon, that made her feel better inside. Kind of like Daddy's whistling made me feel.

Anyway, just lying there gave me time to go over my plan again. This was it. Christmas Eve. I had it all figured out, and Laramie was going to help me. And if I got in trouble for doing it, I figured there was more forgiveness flowing on Christmas Day than any other time of the year. Yep, today was the big day. Christmas Eve dinner at Granny Grace's with the whole family, Christmas Eve service at church, home again, and then I was off to deliver Mama's Christmas present to her.

I didn't hear Uncle Luke or Chesler up and moving around, but the time for lying still was over. I grabbed my robe and my yellow slippers and went downstairs. "Good morning, Daddy." He was rustling Christmas wrapping paper.

"Hey there, little peep. You're up early. You think it's Christmas or something?" He was smiling.

"Almost. No, my head had all the sleep it needed. What are you doing?" I knew he was wrapping presents, but I wanted him to say it.

"Well, with Laramie and now with Lisa, I had a few more presents to wrap."

"Did you get the sketchbook and pencils for Laramie?"

"Yes, they're in my closet. You can wrap them now while she's asleep."

I went to his closet and came back with the bag. "Wow, this is nice. She'll be so happy."

Daddy finished tying a red ribbon on a purple present. He matched ribbons and wrapping paper like Chesler matched his clothes. "I found some special wrapping paper just for you. Look."

He handed me some folded sheets of wrapping paper covered in cardinals sitting on holly branches. "Oh, Laramie'll love this! I told her about Mama and the red-birds." I started wrapping her presents, scrimping with the paper like Aunt Susannah Hope did with the cinnamon in the cider. I wanted to save some, like saving a little bit more of Mama for myself.

Daddy handed me a spool of red ribbon and bundled up all the other wrapping paper and ribbons to store them back in the closet. "Kate, when you finish, let's put these gifts under the tree."

The Christmas tree lights were already plugged in and the room looked like something in one of Aunt Susannah Hope's house decorating magazines. Daddy came in with an armload of boxes right after I did. He put them all around the tree, but he put Laramie's right in the front. "Let's sit down here for a bit and enjoy the lights before everybody else gets up."

I was still moving some of the Christmas presents around. "Can we leave the lights on all day? It's so gray outside."

"Sure we can." Daddy sat down on the sofa. "Kate, there's something important I need to tell you."

I didn't like the sound of that. The only kinds of conversations I ever had with Daddy that started like that were about things I didn't want to hear. I thought about Aunt Susannah Hope and Laramie's dad. "Do I have to hear this, Daddy?"

"Yes, little one, you do, but this is good news. I wanted to talk to you before Laramie gets up." Daddy motioned for me to sit next to him. "But you have to promise me that you won't say a word to Laramie about what I'm telling you. Can you do that?"

"Yes, sir." I curled up next to Daddy on the sofa. I was gladder than glad this wasn't bad news. "You can trust me, Daddy. I am not the blabbermouth in this family."

"That's what I thought. I don't want to tell Laramie because if what I think might happen today doesn't happen, then she'll be one disappointed little girl. But if it does happen, then this will be about the best Christmas of her whole life."

I sat up and looked at Daddy. "What, Daddy? What might happen?"

"Well, it looks like Laramie's mom might be coming home."

"Today?"

"I know. It's almost too good to be true, and I don't want to tell Laramie in case Mrs. Fields can't get here."

I bounced up and down and hugged Daddy. "Laramie's gonna be so happy and so surprised. How'd you find her mom?"

"Well, it's a long story. When Laramie ran away, and her dad went to jail, the sheriff started asking Mr. Fields questions about his wife. Laramie's dad knew where she was but not exactly when or if she would be back."

"But he didn't tell Laramie?"

"No, he didn't. He didn't know what to say, so he just told Laramie she was gone and not to think about her anymore. He didn't even give Laramie the letters her mother wrote to her while she was away."

"That's the meanest thing I ever heard." I hugged my daddy again. "It's hard enough when your mama's not around, but I'm so glad you're my daddy and not Mr. Fields. You were honest when Mama went to heaven."

Daddy kissed me right on top of my head. "I'm glad I'm your daddy too, little peep. We miss your mama, but we're still family." Then Daddy got quiet for a minute. "Laramie's family isn't like ours, Kate. I think you're old enough to understand some of this. Her mom has problems with alcohol. And when she drinks, sometimes she does things she wishes she hadn't done. The last time that happened, Mrs. Fields couldn't face Laramie the next morning, so she left."

"Why couldn't she just talk to Laramie?"

"Sometimes people like Laramie's parents have a hard time admitting and talking about their problems. And I think it was just too hard for her to say good-bye."

"But Laramie woulda felt better if she had known the truth."

"Maybe. That's why she left Laramie a letter explaining that she was going to her sister's in New York, but her dad was so upset, he chose not to give the letter to Laramie. You see, Mrs. Fields decided she wanted to stop drinking so she could be a better mother, but she couldn't do it by herself. The only thing she knew to do was to ask her sister to help her."

"But couldn't she get help here?"

"Maybe, but she needed money, and she needed to be in a hospital to get better and learn how to stay better."

"But how did you get to talk to her?"

"I went to the jail and talked to Mr. Fields. He really does love Laramie and wants his family back, and he didn't want Laramie to spend Christmas without her family. So he told me about his wife and why she left. He said Mrs. Fields's sister knew where she was and gave me her number. So I called the sister, and she told me how to get in touch with Laramie's mom."

"Oh, Daddy, this is so good. Is Mrs. Fields healed now?"

"Well, she's been in a special hospital to help her, and I think she's better now, at least well enough to come home and try to start over with Laramie."

When Mama got sick, everybody was praying for Mama to get healed, but she went to heaven anyway. Daddy said that meant she was healed. And here was Mrs. Fields, and nobody even cared enough to pray for her, and she was alive and in a hospital getting better. Some things didn't make sense to me, but anyway, I was glad Laramie was gonna get her mom back. I just wished Mama was coming with her.

"So when does Mrs. Fields get here?"

"If the weather permits, she'll be here this afternoon. She's traveling a long way, and there could be more snow. Now remember, you can't say a word about this to Laramie just in case her mother doesn't get here, okay?"

Now another secret. I had to walk around all day knowing what might happen that afternoon, and I couldn't tell a soul. I knew how Mama must feel in heaven. "I get it now. Pastor Simmons told me last week that Mama's happy in heaven, even without us, because she knows the end of the story, and one day we'll all be together again."

"What? What are you talking about, and when did you talk to Pastor Simmons?"

Me and my flapping tongue. I didn't need Daddy asking me too many questions today. "Oh, I saw the pastor last Sunday before choir practice, and we were talking about books and stories and happy endings. When we were having hot chocolate after caroling, he came over to me and said he's reading *Charlotte's Web* to his little boy, Harry, all on account of me talking to him."

"You mean I have a smart daughter?"

I wasn't going to say another word about that. "You know when you told me to pray that it wouldn't snow the night you were searching for Laramie?"

"I do. And you must have prayed hard because it quit snowing."

"Well, I'll be walking around praying all day that it doesn't snow again so Mrs. Fields can get here and make a happy ending." I got up. "I'm going to check on Laramie." I left Daddy sitting in front of the Christmas tree. Boy, if he had a calendar, he could put about a million smiley faces on it.

All the way up the stairs I thought about how Laramie's face would look when her mom walked through the front door. I knew I'd never quit smiling if Mama walked through that door.

I asked Granny Grace one time why something so bad happened to Mama and our family when Mama was so good. Granny said she didn't have an answer for that question yet. She said sometimes bad things happen because we bring it on ourselves. I guess that's like what happened at Laramie's house when her mom and dad were doing bad things, and bad things happened.

But Granny said that wasn't what happened with Mama. She said sometimes God just allowed bad things to happen, but He could make some good come of it. I didn't know of one good thing to come of Mama dying yet. I just kept waiting, but I couldn't get mad at Laramie just because her mom might be coming home. Mama wouldn't like that at all.

Then it hit me. If Laramie's mom came, then Laramie wouldn't be here tonight to help me with my plan. I had to think about that.

Laramie must have heard me walk into the room because she turned over and punched at her pillow. "You're already up? What time is it?"

"I haven't been up long. It's just seven-thirty. I think I'm so excited about Christmas and my plan I couldn't sleep." I plopped on the bed.

"Oh, that's right, it's Christmas Eve."

"All day long."

Laramie just lay there on her back and stared at the ceiling. If only I could tell her the end of the story, she'd be jumping up and down all over that bed.

I was so antsy on the inside. "What you thinking about?"

"I don't know."

I propped up on my elbow and looked at her. "You gotta know what you're thinking about. If you don't, then who does?"

"I was just thinking that it's Christmas Eve and I don't have any presents for anybody. Not even you and

your family, and I really want to give Miss Applegate
something."

"Oh, we don't need any presents. Granny Grace and
Aunt Susannah Hope go crazy with presents. Sometimes
I think they just like to wrap things. Besides, I know
you're my friend."

Laramie had been like Granny's dog too. She had
been acting out at school and using bad language
because she was hurting and she was scared. But she
had been on her best behavior and using good manners
while she was at our house because she knew we were
just trying to make her feel better. I couldn't wait to
tell Emily about Laramie's good manners so we could
all be friends.

Laramie got quiet again.

I didn't want her to worry about anything today. "I
just thought of something you could give to somebody
special."

"What? You mean like a real present for Miss
Applegate?"

"Yeah, a real present. You know that redbird you drew
in my sketchbook?"

"Uh-huh."

"I was thinking about finding a frame around here,
and you could put that drawing in it."

Laramie sat up in bed. "Then I could wrap it up and
give it to Miss Lisa. Then maybe she'd give me art lessons with you. You think she would?"

"I think so. Maybe." I got out of bed. "There's got to be
a frame around here somewhere." I didn't like to lie, but
I was thinking about who was really going to getting this
gift. One time Granny said that whatever came out of my

mouth better be true, but sometimes it might not have to be the whole truth. Right now if I told Laramie the whole truth, then I'd be breaking the secret Daddy told me, and that was worse than not telling her everything.

"I would really like to learn how to draw like you, Kate. We could draw together."

"You already can draw, Laramie, but it would be fun to draw together. Now get up. It's Christmas Eve. We have things to do. We're going to Granny's for Christmas Eve dinner tonight, then we're going to church. Then my plan."

"Are you sure about this plan of yours?"

"Yeah, I've been thinking about it all night. I've changed my mind though. I don't think I want you to help me. I mean, this is something I gotta do by myself. And besides, if it doesn't work, then only one of us is in trouble. I'm not scared. I'm gonna do it."

"But I want to go with you."

"I know, but I really think it's best if you don't. You gotta stay behind. You'll know if it works." I was holding my fingers crossed behind my back the whole time because I knew I wasn't telling the whole truth. Here she was, my new best friend, but come tomorrow, she'd know why I told her I had to do it by myself.

We finished dressing, and Laramie picked up the rocks on my desk. "Why do you have these?"

"Mama."

"What do you mean, Mama?"

"She told me before she went to heaven to always remember these three words to keep my head above water. Faith. Family. Forever."

"To keep your head above water? Is that supposed to make sense?" Laramie was brushing her hair.

"Breakfast in ten minutes." Daddy's announcement came from the bottom of the stairs.

"I'll explain it later. Come on, breakfast is almost ready." I didn't feel like talking about it. I didn't know if Laramie had any rocks to stand on like Mama told me. Besides, her mom was coming home. Maybe Mr. Josh was right. At least one story might have a happy ending.

Uncle Luke was helping Daddy when we got to the kitchen. Superspiderman showed up with bed head and without his socks or slippers. Daddy sent him to the bathroom to comb his hair before he came to the table. That boy never learned.

After we ate, Daddy talked about the day and what we'd be doing. "Kate, Granny's coming in a little while. She's bringing your Christmas dress." I didn't grow much this year, so Granny just let down the hem on last year's dress.

Laramie perked up. "I have a Christmas dress. My aunt sent it to me in the mail last week. It's at my house."

"Would you like us to go get it for you?" Uncle Luke looked at Daddy.

"Yes, sir. I know where the spare key is if you would take me there."

Daddy looked back at Uncle Luke. "Well, I'd say that's just perfect. Maybe you could do that right now while Kate and I clean up the kitchen. Laramie, you and Kate will be the two prettiest girls at church tonight."

Uncle Luke snapped to attention. "Sounds good. Get your coat on, Laramie. We'll run get your dress, and then I'll drop you off here because I have some super-secret errands to run."

Superspiderman had a chocolate milk moustache. "For Miss Lisa? Miss Lisa's gonna be my aunt. Then I'll have two aunts."

Uncle Luke patted Chesler's head. "That's right, buddy. So did you grow that brown moustache overnight?"

Chesler did it again, just rubbed chocolate milk on his Superman pajama sleeve. No wonder Daddy said he was thinking of putting a TV in the laundry room. He spent an awful lot of time there.

While Laramie was gone, Daddy found a frame, and I got Laramie's redbird all fixed and wrapped and under the tree. I wrapped it in the redbird paper too.

After Laramie came back, we drew and played games and listened to Christmas music. It was gray all day, and I kept going to the window hoping for sunshine. I wished and prayed every time I looked out that God would hold back the snow again, just one more time, so Laramie's mom could get here. Daddy didn't tell me where she was coming from. I just knew it was far away, and I hoped it wasn't from the north. News said it was snowing north and west of here, and I was getting worried.

Three o'clock, and Mrs. Fields hadn't come yet. At exactly three fifty-two, the phone rang. Daddy came in minutes later with a smile on his face. "Girls, you need to get dressed. It takes you longer. Chesler, hit the tub, buddy. You didn't shower this morning. Uncle Luke and Lisa will be here in about an hour."

"Let's go. You first." I followed behind Laramie, but I turned around to look at Daddy. He was smiling and gave me the thumbs-up sign. That meant she was coming. Laramie's mom was on her way.

My Christmas dress had been hanging on the door-knob all day. Mama made it last year out of green velvet with a red sash. And there were petticoats underneath. I put it on and Laramie helped me button it in the back and tie the sash.

"I'm so glad I'm just giving the welcome and singing in the choir tonight at the pageant. I don't have to wear one of those dumb costumes like Chesler. He's a sheep."

"A sheep's in the Christmas pageant?"

"Yeah, a sheep. Granny Grace and Aunt Susannah Hope glued cotton balls all over a king-sized pillow-case to make it look like sheep's wool. And they took one of my old head bands and glued on floppy ears made out of felt and covered in cotton balls." I laughed out loud. "Granny said his floppy ears make him look like a cross between an old hound dog and a cotton patch."

"Well, your dress is prettier than any costume, Kate."

"Thanks, Mama made it for me last Christmas. Good thing I didn't grow too much this year." I shut the second drawer in my dresser. "I gotta find that big red ribbon. Mama made it too. It goes in my hair a special way." I kept looking. "Here it is, bottom drawer."

I brushed my hair while Laramie put on her dress. I was glad Mama tied that bow, sewed it, and glued it on to the back of a comb so all I had to do was stick it in my hair. Daddy could never fix my hair as nice as Mama did.

I could see Laramie in the mirror behind me, and I turned around. "Oh, how pretty! I love that blue. It looks so pretty with your eyes."

"Thanks. Would you zip it?"

I zipped it. It was a little bit tight. She had on white tights to match the white lace collar. She looked like a doll that belonged under the Christmas tree.

"I have a barrette with white lace and ribbons. You want to wear it?"

"Sure. Is it okay?"

"Of course. You can put it right there on the side where your stitches are, and nobody'll see them."

When we finished, I sprayed a little bit of Mama's perfume on us. Daddy said I could do that on special occasions. And this was a special day.

Uncle Luke and Miss Lisa had just walked in the front door when we came downstairs. Uncle Luke looked at us and then back at Miss Lisa and said, "Three beautiful girls. I'm just glad I don't have to choose which one's the prettiest."

He would choose Miss Lisa. She had on the red lipstick again to match her red Christmas dress.

Daddy had the camera on the tripod set up in the living room. "Okay, time for the Christmas picture, and aren't we glad Lisa and Laramie will be in our family picture this year?"

Uncle Luke started clapping, and Chesler and I did too. Uncle Luke looked like he wanted to kiss Miss Lisa, but I didn't think he was about to kiss that much lipstick, not with all of us watching.

"Chesler, come here. Your tie looks like Grady tied it."

Chesler left his spot and ran to Daddy. "Grady can't tie my tie. He's a hound dog."

"Exactly what I mean." Daddy fixed it and sent him back to his place for the picture. The timer was set. Daddy mashed the button and walked over real fast to stand between me and Chesler. It beeped ten times, and there was our family Christmas photo. Just after it flashed, the doorbell rang.

Chesler took off toward the door, but Daddy caught him just as he rounded the corner of the living room that leads into the front hall. "Wait just a minute. You may be dressed up like the butler, but don't answer the door. I want to take your picture with Uncle Luke and Lisa." He patted Chesler on the behind and sent him back to his place in front of the Christmas tree.

"Laramie?"

"Yes, sir."

"Would you mind getting the door while I take this last photo?"

"No, sir. I mean yes, sir, I'll get it." Laramie walked just like a lady out of that living room.

As soon as her back was turned, Daddy was smiling so big we could count his teeth all the way back to his molars. He motioned for us all to come and stand behind the French door so we could see.

Laramie grabbed the doorknob, and she had to tug on it a couple of times before it would open. On the third tug, that old door came wide open. Laramie just stood there like some kind of statue, holding on to that doorknob like she might fall down if she let go. "Mom?"

"Yes, Laramie, it's me."

"Really, it's you?"

That's when Laramie's mom came through that door, and Laramie cried and hugged her and held her the way I hugged Mama the night she went to heaven, just like she wasn't ever letting her go. She was so pretty, blonde and green-eyed just like Laramie. Then Mr. Fields came in too, and all three of them hugged each other all over again.

Daddy led us all into the front hall to meet Mr. and Mrs. Fields. He introduced everyone. Mrs. Fields must have thanked him about a million times for taking care of her sweet girl. I took Laramie upstairs to get her things while they talked.

When they were saying good-bye, I remembered my Christmas present for Laramie and the other present. "Wait just a minute. I have to get something."

Daddy must have invited them over for our family Christmas because when I got back to the front hall, Mrs. Fields was saying they really should have their own Christmas and not intrude on ours.

I handed Laramie's present to her. "Here, Laramie, this is from me."

She hugged me and thanked me.

"And here's the present you made for your mom." I handed her the other present wrapped up in redbird paper.

"But, I…"

I stretched my eyes and shook my head. Then she smiled and her face told me she understood. She took the present from my hand.

Laramie's mom took her hand. "Let's go, Laramie. We have lots of things to talk about and some explaining to do." Then she thanked Daddy for all he did to help their family. Even Mr. Fields shook Daddy's hand. I could tell he didn't have words.

Before she left, Laramie hugged me one last time, and I whispered in her ear, "Go be with your mom and dad. You're gonna have the best Christmas ever."

"Kate, I love you. I hope your plan works."

"It'll work. It's just got to."

CHAPTER EIGHTEEN

CHRISTMAS MUSIC PLAYED, and Granny had candles lit everywhere when she met us at the back door with her red Christmas apron on.

My aunt and uncle were already there. Aunt Susannah had a little more color in her cheeks than when I saw her last time at the hospital. She asked, "Where's Laramie?"

Daddy told her the whole story about Laramie's mom coming home. My aunt just cried. I knew she was missing Mama and wishing she'd come walking through that door just like Laramie's mom did. Whenever Mama walked into a room, everybody looked, and just seeing her put a smile on their faces.

Last Christmas Eve was our first one without Grandpa, and now Mama's chair at the table was empty too. Made me look around the room and think about what could happen by next Christmas. But if I knew Granny, she wouldn't allow too much time for being sad tonight.

Everybody was in the kitchen, the way they always were at Granny's house.

Granny switched off the griddle. "Susannah Hope, look at Lisa's hand and see what happened when she and Luke were out here skating on the pond last night." Aunt Susannah Hope was probably expecting a cast on Miss Lisa's arm the way Granny talked. She was so surprised when she saw that ring that she started crying all over again.

Granny gave everybody a job except Chesler. His job was to stay out of the way until the food was on the table. When we were all in our seats, Granny Grace asked Uncle Don to pray. He prayed good prayers, but they could be long. I opened my eyes and looked around. Granny was sitting in Grandpa's seat at the end of the table. Miss Lisa was sitting in Granny's old seat next to Uncle Luke, and I was in Mama's chair right next to Daddy. I closed my eyes again when I thought he was about to say amen.

Granny's supper was simple compared to what our Christmas lunch would be tomorrow. Every Christmas Eve since I could remember, we've sat around Granny's dining table with her red Christmas cloth on it. We have the same thing—French onion soup, grilled cheese sandwiches on my aunt's homemade bread, and fruit salad. Daddy insisted on making the fruit salad this year because that was always Mama's job.

Grandpa used to grumble, "Gracie, I don't know why you have to serve cheese on top of the soup, and another half a pound of cheese on my sandwich. You know that much cheese messes up my plumbing." The first time I heard him say that, I just laughed because everybody else did. But when Daddy explained it to me about the plumbing and all, I laughed out loud all over again.

When we finished our supper, Granny, Aunt Susannah, and Miss Lisa cleared the table, and Granny brought out the Santa Claus platter of her homemade cookies and fudge. "Okay, just a reminder, if you eat all these cookies tonight, you won't get any tomorrow." She always said that too.

Then came my favorite part, not because of the cookies, but because Granny brought out the magic marker, and we all signed our names on the table cloth again. The table was cleared of dishes, so we could see everybody's names from years ago. I was looking for how Mama signed her name when she was in the second grade. She signed it "llennoD'O yoJ anaiD" just to be different. And then one year she drew smiley faces in all the Os in her name. We always laughed about that. Granny made a big deal about Miss Lisa signing her name for the first time. One time Granny told me that when she went to heaven she wanted me to have the Christmas tablecloth.

We put on our coats to leave for the Christmas Eve service, and Aunt Susannah Hope insisted Granny ride with them. Granny refused. "I'm riding in the car with these young folks. I need to make sure Chesler and Kate know their lines for the Christmas program. But go ahead and put my overnight bag in your car. I'm spending the night in town with you and Don. Oh, where's Chesler's sheep costume?"

Uncle Don was helping my aunt to get in the car. "It's in our car, and your bag's already there too. Anything else you need?"

"No. We'll come back early in the morning for the food I've prepared and for all the presents. That is, we'll get the presents if these children are good tonight." Granny smiled.

I knew she didn't mean that. She'd be giving presents no matter what. She was asking me to say my lines before we got down the lane to the main road. I said them perfect the first time. Then she insisted Chesler sing his solo. Asking Chesler to sing is like mashing the "on" button of a radio. He had us all singing Christmas songs by the time we got to town.

"Now you two kids sing like that tonight, and your mama and your grandpa will be clapping all the way from heaven."

Uncle Luke had Chesler in his lap in the back seat. "And your dad and I will jump up and yell just like we do at the baseball game."

"Nah, you can't do that, Uncle Luke, not if Granny's sitting next to you. She pinches." Everybody laughed at Chesler.

Daddy parked in the lot across the street from the church, and we all got out. "Would you look at that? That's one beautiful old church." The church ladies on the decorating committee had tied red ribbons to the iron fence around the old stone church, and candlelight shone from the windows.

Daddy slapped Uncle Luke across the shoulder. "You sure you don't want a Christmas wedding?"

"Not on your life. If Lisa wants snow, then I'll bring in a snow-making machine. But we're getting married right here in June. Right, Lisa?"

"Right. With white rose petals, who needs snow? And with Chesler and Kate, looks like we have our singer, and I have a bridesmaid."

"I'm so excited to be a bridesmaid. Thank you, Miss Lisa." I took her hand. "Would it be okay if I started calling you Aunt Lisa?"

She squeezed my hand. "You know, I think I'd like that a whole lot. I've been waiting a long time to be an aunt."

Granny hung on to Daddy's arm when we crossed the street. Pastor Simmons was standing at the door to greet us. He asked about Laramie. Daddy didn't get to tell him everything about Laramie's mom, just that she was home and he was hopeful everything would work out for that family. "And speaking of families, Luke, here, will be asking you to tie the knot to start another family right here in June." Daddy took Aunt Lisa's hand and showed the pastor her engagement ring.

"Yes, sir. Lisa and I'll be coming in next week to talk to you about the wedding. We can't imagine getting married anywhere else."

Pastor Simmons shook Uncle Luke's hand. "Now that's plain beautiful, Luke. One of my favorite things about being a pastor is the sweet time I have with families at weddings and funerals."

I agreed weddings were "plain beautiful," but funerals? Maybe that was another one of those things I'd understand better when I grew up.

"Two services tonight, Pastor?" Granny asked.

"Oh, yes. This one with the children's pageant, and then there's another one at eleven."

"Too late for my blood." Granny moved on over by Uncle Luke.

The pastor turned to me. "Kate, I think the other kids are gathering in the choir room. You and Chesler better hurry." Then he reached for the basket and started handing out candles to the grown-ups. "And the rest of you, don't forget your candles, you'll need them for the end of the service."

Aunt Susannah went with us to make sure Chesler put on his costume right.

It wasn't long before Mrs. Crouch cranked up that organ and made it sound like trumpets. That was our signal to come out and take our places. The choir for adults was behind us in the choir loft, and we were on risers out front. All the kids in costumes were in the manger scene over by the organ.

I came out with Pastor Simmons and stood beside him while he welcomed everybody to the church. I looked around, hoping to see Laramie and her parents. Daddy was sitting between Granny and Aunt Susannah Hope. On the other side of Granny, Uncle Luke and Aunt Lisa were sitting like they were glued together. Miss Evie was sitting down front with the pastor's wife, her blond hair shining in the candlelight.

After the pastor said his welcome, he turned to me. "And now, Miss Katherine Joy Harding will announce our Christmas pageant."

I was right in the middle of my four lines when I saw Laramie and Mr. and Mrs. Fields come in and sit in the back row. She waved at me, and I waved back just a little and finished my lines. From the look on Granny's face, I did a good job.

Emily got the biggest part in the pageant this year. Her part was to read the story while the characters in costume acted it out. And at the right time, the choir would sing a song, and then everybody would clap.

Everything went along fine. Emily read her words clear and loud, and everybody remembered the words to the songs. Then came Chesler's turn to sing his solo.

He stepped away from the manger scene and stood in the middle of the stage, out in front of everybody. He looked like Grady covered in cotton balls. His ears were lopsided because he let the headband slip. But when that boy opened his mouth to sing, nobody thought about floppy ears or cotton balls. He closed his eyes, and what came out of his mouth sounded like Mama, just like it came from heaven. His voice was clear as a bell. And you could understand every word.

> Christmas is heaven come to earth.
> Lives changed forever with this Baby's birth.
> All is well, no need to fear.
> Heaven's in Christmas, for Jesus is here.
> Peace has come; all is well;
> Peace is His presence in us to dwell.
> All is well; all is well.

All this time I thought it kinda strange that a little boy sheep would be singing "All Is Well." But tonight, for the first time, it made sense. Because of what Emily had read moments ago from the book of Isaiah:

> *The wolf will live with the lamb,*
> *the leopard will lie down with the goat,*
> *the calf and the lion and the yearling together;*
> *and a little child will lead them.*

That was going to be some kind of day when that happened. I guessed that was the end of the story that Mama knew, when God made everything all right.

I looked at Daddy, and he and Granny both were smiling and crying at the same time. When Chesler sang his last note, he just stood there like he had to wait until his soul came back to his body. And then he opened his eyes.

But not one person clapped. Not one.

I wondered if angel wings were fluttering all over that old church. Chesler, floppy ears and all, went back to his place and sat down at the manger scene.

The last thing on the program was the lighting of the candles. The ushers turned out all the lights, only they didn't blow out the candles in the windows. Pastor Simmons talked about light coming into a dark world on Christmas, and then he lit his candle from the Christ candle on the altar table. He told us to keep our candles burning until we got to our cars and to leave in silence. When we sang "Silent Night," he started lighting the candle of the person at the end of every row. That was really something with everybody holding up candles in the darkness.

All the people got up out of their pews and walked up the aisle toward the door. Pastor Simmons was at the door still holding his candle and saying quietly, "Peace be with you and merry Christmas," to everybody.

It was snowing a little when we walked outside. I held my hand around my candle to keep the wind from blowing it out. The pastor said to leave in silence, and most folks did. But when we got to our car, it was like the Booster Club for the high school football team was waiting on Chesler. That boy got more hugs and kisses and little old women crying over his singing.

Daddy had just cranked up the car when he saw Mrs. Crouch running down the sidewalk. "Wait, John, just wait." She slowed down when she saw Daddy roll down his window. "Thanks, John, these organ shoes are going to be the death of me on this ice. I need to speak with Chesler."

Mrs. Crouch took off her glasses and stuck her head in the window where Daddy was sitting. "Chesler, I couldn't let you get away without telling you that was the most beautiful singing I've ever heard in all of my seventy-six years, sweet boy. I didn't want you to be upset because nobody clapped."

Chesler got a look on his face like this was news to him.

"Oh, child, the reason nobody clapped is because it was just so beautiful no one could move. No one could have even whispered after you finished singing; it would just have destroyed that special moment they didn't want to end."

Daddy turned around to look at Chesler. "What do you say to Mrs. Crouch, Chesler?"

"Thank you, Mrs. Crouch."

"John, you should be button-popping proud of both your children. And one of these days I know I'm going to look over the organ into the choir, and you'll be back in your seat." She pinched Daddy's cheek just like he was a little boy. "I hope you Hardings have a very merry Christmas."

"And merry Christmas to you too, Mrs. Crouch."

I was watching Mrs. Crouch waddle back to the church when I spotted Laramie. "Daddy, there's Laramie. Can I just go tell her good night?"

"Sure, but hurry."

I opened the car door and nearly skidded across the parking lot to catch up with Laramie and her mom. They were walking arm in arm, with Mr. Fields just ahead. I whispered loud since we were supposed to be silent. "Hey, Laramie, wait up."

She turned around and saw me. "Hi, Kate."

"I just wanted to say merry Christmas. Sure wish you and your mom and dad would come for Christmas lunch tomorrow. Granny'll have enough food to feed everybody. Won't you come?"

She turned to her mother. "Can we, Mom? Granny Grace cooks good."

"Please, Mrs. Fields, please. You just have to come. My family has more presents for Laramie."

"Okay, let's do it. I don't think I can say no to you girls on Christmas Eve. What time?"

"It's Sunday, so we come to church at eleven, then home for lunch. Want to meet us for church?"

"We'll see you then. And tell your granny I'll be bringing a dish." Mrs. Fields opened the car and got in.

Laramie came closer and whispered, "You still going through with your plan tonight?"

"Yeah. Would you say a prayer for me that it'll work?"

"I will. I'm sorry I don't get to help you." Laramie hugged me like a sister.

"Thanks, but it's something I really need to do myself. See you tomorrow."

I walked back to the car and climbed in. "Guess who's coming to lunch tomorrow?"

Uncle Luke had it all figured out. "Wouldn't be Laramie and her parents, would it?"

Chesler clapped. He liked Laramie now.

Daddy said, "It'll be good to have extra folks around the table, then we won't be eating Christmas leftovers until New Year's."

When we got home, Uncle Luke took Daddy's car and drove Aunt Lisa home. Daddy told Chesler and me to put on our pajamas and we could watch television for a little while. When it was almost ten o'clock, Daddy said it was time for all good children to be in bed.

So we headed upstairs like Daddy said. When we got to the top of the stairs, Chesler whispered, "You still gonna take Mama's present to her tonight?"

"Yeah, go to bed and be quiet so Daddy'll think we're asleep. I'll come to your room in a little while." Just one time I hoped he'd do what I told him. He'd better.

I went to my room and closed the door and climbed into bed. I didn't think of any of the sweet things Mama told me to think about when I couldn't go to sleep because I had to stay awake. I heard Uncle Luke come in, and then he and Daddy came upstairs. Daddy opened my door just to check on me. He closed it when he thought I was asleep. I hope Chesler pretended as well as I did.

When I didn't hear anything else for a little while, I got up and peeked out my door. All the bedroom doors were closed, and the lights were out. I got my flashlight from under my bed and the scissors out of my desk drawer and laid them on my dresser. Before Mama went to heaven, she gave me her sewing box. Sometimes I sat at my desk and tried on her thimble and looked at all the thread and buttons and pieces of ribbon and lace. Mama said I was old enough to have her good scissors, and I was glad because I needed good scissors tonight.

I went to my closet and pulled out the toy chest Grandpa made me. I needed to stand on it to reach the box I painted for Mama. It was hidden behind my old dolls on the top shelf. I fished it out and put it on the dresser.

Mama taught me to brush my hair every night, so I did that next, wishing I had Mama's hair. Everybody talked about Diana Joy Harding's hair. Hers was long and dark red and curly and shiny, but I got Daddy's hair, brown and straight.

I looked in the mirror and pulled my hair over my shoulder. Then I took Mama's sewing scissors and snipped a lock of hair. I tied the hair with a piece of red ribbon from Mama's sewing basket, then I put it in the red box and closed the lid. Mama would like this.

I put on my clothes, three layers to stay warm. At eleven fifteen I crept out my door and took the red box and scissors and a marker and went to Chesler's room.

He was still awake. I turned on the lamp next to his bed and put the box on his flannel sheets.

"Just sit up, Chesler. You don't have to get out of bed." I knew if he got out of bed, he'd make noise and Daddy would come.

"But I have to get up to put my clothes on. I'm going with you. I'm gonna do Laramie's part." At least he whispered.

"No, you're not going with me. You're staying here. Now just sit up and be quiet."

"Kate, you can't go by yourself. You know what Daddy would say."

"So, what do you think he would say if I took you with me? You're not going, Chesler, and that's final."

"But why can't you just put Mama's present under the tree like everybody else's?"

"Chesler, just think about it. Mama's in heaven. She's not coming by here tonight like Santa Claus to pick up her present and eat the cookies we left. I have to take it to church. God'll be there, and I've been asking Him to take this gift to Mama."

"But it's dark and cold outside. Aren't you scared?"

"Maybe a little, but I have a flashlight, and there'll be people at church for the candlelight service. Now be still just for a minute."

He pulled his head away. "Is this going to hurt?"

"Does it hurt when Daddy takes you to the barbershop?" Before he knew what happened, I snipped a couple of his red curls. He'd never miss them. "Now did that hurt?"

"No, but I don't want to do it again. This was just for Mama."

"I know. Just for Mama."

I handed him the note and the marker. "Here, sign this while I tie the ribbon." I wrote the note myself. It said,

> *Merry Christmas, Mama.*
>
> *We didn't know what to get you for Christmas. Daddy says heaven is such a wonderful place that you don't need anything. So Chesler and I are giving you locks of our hair like you gave to Granny Grace. That way we'll be close to you forever.*
>
> *Love,*
> *Katherine Joy and Chesler*
>
> *PS I see the redbird all the time in the cedar tree, Mama.*
> *Faith. Family. Forever.*

I put the note back in the box, tied the last piece of ribbon around it, and grabbed the flashlight from Chesler's bedside table. "Now I gotta go. I have to get there before the service is over or I won't even be able to get in the church."

"Tell me again how you're going to do it. Will you be back so Santa Claus can come?"

I told him my plan again. "Yes, Chesler, I'll be back so Santa Claus will come."

"But aren't you going to pray while you're there?"

"Yeah, and you pray too. Mama said God answers prayers, and I just know He would want Mama to be happy this Christmas. Now go to sleep, and I'll be back before the bumblebees buzz in the blossoms."

Chesler giggled. "That's what Mama used to say."

"Yeah, that's what Mama used to say." I turned out the light and tiptoed down the stairs. The grandfather clock in the front hall was chiming eleven-thirty when I tucked the box underneath my sweater and put on my heavy coat. I made sure the front door wasn't locked when I closed it behind me.

CHAPTER NINETEEN

*T*HE COLD WIND was blowing sideways, and my jacket was barely slowing it down. Granny Grace called this kind of night bone chilling. I only had to climb the hill to get to the main road, then around the corner past Aunt Susannah Hope's house, and then a few more blocks to the square. I covered up my face with my scarf and started walking. The moon was so bright on the snow I didn't need my flashlight. It would really be all right with me if the wind would stop blowing so hard though.

I hadn't walked too far when I could see the lights from the traffic on the main road up ahead. When I got to the top of the hill, there was a streetlight on the corner. I hid in the bushes for a few minutes until the cars stopped coming by. With a full moon, the streetlight, and the Christmas lights all down the street, somebody might see me.

I walked right past Aunt Susannah Hope's house. It looked like it was raining Christmas bulbs all the way around her front porch, and that big old pine tree in the living room window shined like it was the only Christmas tree on the whole block. The lights were still on, and it would be like Granny and my aunt to be in the kitchen finishing up the last dishes for tomorrow's

Christmas lunch. If they knew I was out this late by myself, I'd be in time-out the rest of my life.

I kept walking and ducking in the bushes whenever I saw car lights. The Wilson's house was completely dark except for the trail of white smoke coming from the chimney. I didn't have to worry about their dog barking at me. He'd be inside on a night like tonight. Just three more blocks to the corner and then two blocks to the church.

I thought about Laramie being out in the cold all by herself for so long before she showed up at our house Monday night. And she was hurt, and she didn't know what was going to happen to her. All I had to do was get to the church and hide until the service was over. At least it'd be warm in there, and then I could go back home. I wished Laramie was with me, but she didn't need any more trouble right now.

I could hear the organ when I was a half a block away from the church. Good. The service was under way. There were no folks in sight when I got there. They were still singing and nobody could hear or see me, so I opened the door, slipped in, and headed down the side hallway out of sight. It was dark, and no one would come this way 'cause the bathrooms and the pastor's office were down the other hall.

I brushed the snow off and took off my earmuffs. I might be the only creature stirring in this hallway on the night before Christmas, but I still tiptoed. I ducked in the first classroom to wait for "Silent Night," my signal to get ready 'cause the service would soon be over. All I had to do was wait. I didn't move a muscle and wished I were invisible. Any minute Pastor Simmons would say,

"Let us go and carry God's light into the darkness." Then everybody would light their candles and head to the parking lot. The wind was blowing so hard, they'd be hurrying to their cars. Then I could do what I came to do and get home.

The way I had things figured, when everybody was out the door, Pastor Simmons would go back to his office and hang up his robe. And I'd have time to take Mama's present to the altar table and say my prayer. I'd be out that front door before he came back in to turn out the lights and lock up and set the alarm.

So I waited and waited for the people to leave, and then I heard somebody say, "Pastor, you better lock up. Just saw some old vagabond walking up the street." I was standing ready to take off down the hall when every-thing went dark, and I heard the front door close and the click of metal.

It was dark and quiet, and I kept waiting for the pastor to come back in, but he didn't. I was so quiet I could hear my eyes batting. I don't know how long I waited, but it finally came to me that he wasn't coming back. I was locked in the church all by myself.

I shivered. How was I gonna get out and get home? Mama and Daddy didn't like me to be anywhere by myself, but I guessed if I had to be somewhere by myself, the church was a good place, especially on Christmas Eve. Still, I was glad Chesler wasn't with me. He'd be whining by now.

I came out from behind the door and tiptoed down the hall to the front entrance, quiet as a cat. I didn't know why I was so quiet. There was no one there to hear me, and there was no light in the front hall. "Dark as Egypt," Granny would say. Now I knew what she meant.

I checked the door. It was locked and the alarm was set, and I didn't have a key. I walked down the hall to Pastor Simmons's office. His door was locked. That meant I couldn't even get to a phone to call Daddy. I turned around and went through the doorway into where we had church. No lights there either, except the red letters of the exit sign at the side door and the streetlights shining through the stained glass windows. The room was still warm, but it wouldn't stay that way long unless they left the heat on for tomorrow morning's services. At least I was out of the wind, and I was safe because the door was locked.

I stood in the aisle. My eyes were getting used to the dark. The church was real quiet like Mama's sewing room, and it looked big and empty in the dark, but I had my flashlight.

Chesler promised he wouldn't tell anyone about my plan, but he never kept his promises. If I wasn't home in the morning, he'd tell Daddy where I was, and they'd come and find me. Daddy would be so happy I was okay that maybe he wouldn't be too mad. He wouldn't let me miss Christmas. But if this was the one time Chesler decided to keep his promise, then I'd be stranded here until folks started coming to church in the morning.

My flashlight stuck out of my coat pocket, just waiting for me to turn it on and walk down the aisle, so I did. I went over to the side door to check it out. I thought about pushing it to see if it would open. But that would set the alarm off, and the police would come.

I didn't know what else to do, so I sat down on the pew and started thinking. But then I heard something, a creaking sound and the wind howling. Those old church walls sure made some strange noises. I put my earmuffs back on so I couldn't hear. The streetlights shined through the stained glass, and the tree limbs nearby made shadows on the windows. I shut my eyes so tight it seemed they might never open again. I couldn't see or hear. I had never been in an empty church before, and it felt like being in the cemetery. And then I thought of Laramie being all by herself and hurt and hiding in the shed out back of the school. She must have been so scared.

I didn't like being here all by myself, but I'd rather stay here all night alone and have Daddy find me in the morning than have the police take me home in the middle of the night on Christmas Eve. Everybody in town would be talking about that little Harding girl.

Finally I decided I might as well do what I came here to do, so I got up and walked to the altar table and put my flashlight down next to the advent wreath. I unbuttoned my coat and reached under my sweater for the special box. Holding it in my hands like I was holding on to Mama, I knelt down on the floor right in front of the Christ candle, wishing it was lit.

"Dear God," I prayed, "I've been telling You it's real important that my mama gets this for Christmas. I know she's got everything she needs in heaven and all, but I think she'd really like to have this. She can keep it with her until I get there. Please God, I didn't mean to get locked in the church. That wasn't part of my plan. I'm sorry if I'm in trouble, but I just didn't know where else to take Mama's present. I knew You'd be here. And God, if there's ever a time Chesler keeps his promise, please don't let it be now. Please let Daddy find me and not be too mad. I don't like being all by myself in here, and I'm real scared, God. Oh, and thank You for the redbird You send to the cedar tree. She reminds me of Mama. Amen."

I got up and placed Mama's gift on the altar table next to the Christ candle. Just as I put it down, there was a strange noise like a rumble. I hoped it was the wind blowing hard, but it didn't sound like that. I was too scared to turn around, and I wanted to scream, but I didn't think anything would come out. I searched for my flashlight on the table and found it. With my other hand I removed my earmuffs. And then I heard it. Someone clearing his throat.

"Good evening, Katherine Joy." His voice was scraggly like he needed to cough or clear his throat again.

Whoever it was knew me, and I had heard that voice before, but where? I held tight to my flashlight.

"I heard you praying. I hope you don't mind."

I knew his voice, and I turned around to see. Light coming through the stain-glassed windows made his face look like a kaleidoscope of colors. "Mr. Josh?" I looked harder. "Mr. Josh, is that really you?"

He was holding his wool cap in his hands. "I'm right here, and it makes me so happy you remembered me."

"I remember you from the hospital, but what are you doing here?" I asked.

"Oh, I was just passing through and needed a warm place to spend the night."

"But I didn't think anyone else was here. I thought I was locked in all alone." I wanted to hug him, but I didn't.

"Well, I'm here too. I know, little one, the church is empty most of the time." He rubbed his hand across his scruffy beard. "You know why I'm here, and I heard your prayer, so I know why you're here." He stepped closer to the table and ran his finger over the top of the red box.

If he took Mama's present, I didn't know what I'd do.

"Why don't we light this candle?"

Then he reached under his coat, and I could see he still had on that old gray wool sweater. Just like at the hospital, he pulled out that green book of matches with Haven of Hope on it, and he lit the Christ candle. "Maybe with this candle burning, you'll see you're not alone."

His voice was real gentle, and I wasn't so scared anymore. "Why don't we just sit down right here on this pew and look at the flame?" He sat down, and I sat down too, but not too close.

We sat in silence until I couldn't be quiet any longer. "I didn't mean to get locked in here."

Then he said, "I know you didn't. It's a strange thing about the church. The doors are locked from the outside—locked doors for those folks who need to come in because they're out there standing in the cold and the dark. And here you are on the inside, and you don't seem to be able to get out." Then he got quiet again.

"But I really need to go home so my daddy won't be worried."

"Yes, Katherine Joy, daddies like yours tend to do that. It's because he loves you so much, but I don't want you to worry."

"But I can't help it." I just wanted to cry.

"I'm sorry about this mess you think you're in, but everything will be just fine come morning, you'll see. Yes, little one, I think this story will have a happy ending."

Then I remembered, and just for a minute I wasn't sad or worried. "That's what you said at the hospital. My friend, Laramie, her story had a real happy ending. Her mom came home today."

"She did, did she? Well, just maybe that's a happy beginning. Let's see, you've already told me about your mama when we met at the hospital. Seems I remember she was good at singing. Did she come to church here?"

"Yes, sir. You see the chairs in the choir?"

"I do."

I pointed to Mama's seat. "That was where Mama sat. She sat right in the middle on the front row, and she could sing like a redbird."

"Like a redbird, you say? I think I'm familiar with how redbirds sing."

We sat for a little while and watched the candle and the flickers of light coming through the windows.

Then he started singing "Away in a Manger" real quiet like he was singing to himself. His voice sounded like the hinges on my closet door.

I stared at the candle. It was burning so bright in the darkness that it seemed to fill up the cracks of those cold, stone walls and made the wooden pews look warm. I yawned real big. I was getting so sleepy, but I didn't want to say so 'cause I didn't think it was right for me to go to sleep all by myself with this stranger nearby. What if he took Mama's present?

Then he said out of the clear blue like he could read my mind, "It'll be all right if you'd like to go to sleep, Kate. I'll just sit here for a while and look at the candle. Just remember, you're not alone."

I put my feet up on the pew and lay on my side with my arm curled up under my head. My eyelids were so heavy when I lay down on that pew. Mr. Josh just sat there all peaceful like with his arms folded, looking at the candle and humming to himself. I watched him till I just couldn't keep my eyes open any longer.

I don't know how much time passed, but the next thing I knew someone was calling my name.

"Katherine Joy! Kate, are you in here? It's Daddy." I thought I was dreaming until I opened my eyes and saw streaks of red and blue and green morning light pouring in through the church windows. I sat up. There in the aisle was Daddy, and behind him, the pastor and Uncle Luke and Chesler.

"I'm here, Daddy. I'm right here."

The next thing I knew, Daddy was squeezing me, and asking, "Katherine Joy, are you all right?"

I wrapped my arms so tight around Daddy's neck. His beard was scratchy, but I didn't care. "Yes, sir, I'm fine," I said to Daddy. "I'm just fine."

Uncle Luke said, "When you weren't in your room this morning, Chesler told us about your plan."

Chesler climbed up on the pew next to me and tried to hug me. "I had to tell him, Kate. Don't be mad at me. I had to tell Daddy. It's Christmas, and we had to come and find you."

I gave my brother the biggest hug. "It's okay, Chesler. I prayed last night you wouldn't keep your promise. God just answered my prayer."

Daddy patted Chesler on the head. "You did the right thing, son." Then Daddy took my hand and helped me stand up. He looked at me like he hadn't seen me in forty forevers. "What in the world made you come here last night, Kate? Chesler said something about a present for your mama."

"It was the only way for Mama to get her Christmas present."

"What? What about your mama's Christmas present?" Daddy just hugged me tight, and I thought he was going to cry. "Never mind, we'll straighten all that out when we get home, but right now I think you owe the pastor an explanation and an apology. It's Christmas morning, and he had to leave his family to help me find you."

"I'm so sorry. I was just gonna slip in and leave Mama's present before you locked the doors last night, but I got locked in. I didn't mean to worry anybody. I'm so sorry you had to leave your family and Miss Evie and get out in the cold just for me."

Pastor Simmons looked me straight in the face. "Kate, that's one fine apology, and I accept it. But would you mind telling me about this plan of yours?"

"Yes, sir...I mean, no, sir, I don't mind. Do you remember when I came to see you and asked about how I could get Mama's Christmas present to her?"

"Yes, I remember that conversation well. But I don't recall telling you how to do that."

"No, sir, you didn't. Nobody could tell me. But I figured it out for myself. I thought if I could just get Mama's present to the church on Christmas Eve that God would take care of it. I knew He would understand. So I put it right over there on the table."

We all turned to look down at the altar. My eyes grew about as big as Granny's embroidery hoop. Mama's present was gone, and the candle had burned out.

Pastor looked too. "Don't tell me I left that candle burning all night. I could have burned the church down. You didn't light it, did you, Kate?"

"No, sir. I don't have any matches. Daddy doesn't allow us to strike matches." Then I remembered Mr. Josh. I jumped up. "Mama's present was right there. I promise it was. Right there." I touched the place on the table where it had been. "Mr. Josh must have taken it."

Daddy took my shoulder and turned me around. "Mr. Josh? Who's Mr. Josh?"

"I don't know. He's just Mr. Josh. He's an old man, and he was hiding in the church 'cause he needed a warm place to spend the night. He talked to me about Mama, and he lit the candle, and he sang until I fell asleep."

Daddy talked in his real serious voice. "Slow, down, Katherine Joy. You mean to tell me there was someone with you here last night?"

"Yes, sir, Daddy. Mr. Josh was here. I met him at the hospital when we went to visit Laramie. He was right here. We sat together right here on this pew 'til I fell asleep."

Uncle Luke took my hand. "Kate, if he was here, where is he now? He couldn't have gotten out. The doors were locked when we got here. No one was here with you, sweetie. You must have dreamed it."

I looked at Daddy. "I didn't dream it, Daddy. He was here. I promise he was."

I saw the way Pastor Simmons looked at Daddy. "Well, Zack Wheeler told me there was a vagabond walking around the church yard last night. But, John, you know the alarm system was on when I unlocked the doors this morning. No one could have left this building without triggering it. But just to be safe, I'll check my office and the back door and the windows back there. John, you check the hallway where the classrooms are. Luke, maybe you should check the restrooms. Maybe he's still here and hiding."

"I'll help. I know what he looks like. He's got on a long coat, and he has white hair. Come on, Chesler."

"Katherine Joy, you sit right here on this pew with your brother until we get back. Do you understand me? Neither of you move one muscle."

"But Daddy, it's okay. Mr. Josh won't hurt a flea. He took care of me last night."

"You heard me." Daddy and Uncle Luke and Pastor Simmons left the room.

Chesler squirmed over next to me. "Was Mr. Josh for real, Kate? You're not just making this up?"

"I couldn't make up anything like that. No, Chesler, he was for real. If he wasn't for real, where did the present go?"

"I wish I woulda come with you to see him."

"I wish you had been here too, little brother. Then they wouldn't think I'm making this up."

Daddy and Uncle Luke and the pastor walked back in the sanctuary together talking. Pastor Simmons came over and knelt down in front of me. "Kate, whoever you think was here is not to be found in this church, and there doesn't seem to be a way he could have gotten out of the building. But it's okay. Maybe you just had a dream that seemed so real, or maybe it was just your imagination because you were so scared."

I knew Mr. Josh was real. I didn't have that good of an imagination. "Yes, sir, I was scared all right, so maybe he wasn't for real." I didn't need to say anything else 'cause my plan had worked. "Daddy, can we just go home?"

"That's a good idea, Kate, then Pastor Simmons can get back to his family."

Chesler and I walked up the aisle toward the door. I heard Pastor Simmons tell Daddy not to worry. He said that children sometimes invented stories to stay out of trouble, like my daddy didn't already know that. That's when Uncle Luke asked him, "So, I get all that, but what happened to the box?"

Pastor said, "Oh, she just probably dropped it. It'll turn up around here somewhere."

Daddy didn't say a word about all that, but he did some more fussing on the ride home. "Kate, I don't know what I would have done if something happened to you. You can't pull any more stunts like this, wandering around in the streets at midnight. Do you understand?"

"Yes, sir, Daddy, I'm so sorry, and I promise I won't do anything to make you worry ever again in my whole life." Then we just stopped talking.

Daddy parked the car in the garage, and we went in the back door. He stopped in the kitchen. "Okay, I don't think we should say anything about this to Granny Grace or Aunt Susannah Hope today. Do you understand? Not a word."

"You got it, Daddy. Not one word." Chesler zipped his lips.

I nodded but kept my head down. Daddy lifted my chin.

"So tell me, Kate, what did you give your mama?"

"I cut a lock of my hair, and I cut Chesler's too, and put it in a red box. It's just like what Granny Grace has, a lock of Mama's hair. That way, me and Chesler can be with Mama forever."

I saw tears in Daddy's eyes, and he hugged Chesler and me. He was having a hard time talking. "Remember, we'll just keep this to ourselves. Maybe after Christmas, you can tell Granny Grace and Aunt Susannah, but I don't think it's a good idea to upset them on Christmas Day with such a tale."

"Thanks, Daddy, for not making me be in trouble, and I won't say a word."

Uncle Luke shouted, "Anybody ready to see if Santa Claus made a stop by here last night?"

Chesler nearly knocked me over trying to get to the Christmas tree in the living room. He just threw his jacket down on the floor of the front hall and took off.

Daddy picked up Chesler's jacket and hung it on the hall tree and hugged me again. "I'm just so glad you're okay. Let's open some presents." He walked into the living room.

I took off my mittens and stuck them in my left coat pocket. And as I reached into my right coat pocket to pull out my flashlight, something fell from my pocket onto the floor. I picked it up. A book of matches! I ran my fingers over the green cover. Printed in gold letters, it read Haven of Hope. Mr. Josh's matches.

I just smiled and put the matchbook in my jeans pocket. It was Christmas, the season of miracles, and Mr. Josh had told me everything would turn out good. And it had.

Chapter Twenty

Santa Claus had made a stop at the Harding house, and from the looks of the floor around the tree, he emptied his whole sleigh full of gifts right there in our living room. Chesler was at work, and Christmas paper was flying around the room like Granny pitching hay in her barn.

Chesler opened his presents first, jumping up and down when he saw his new cassette player and skates and rod and reel. "Just what I wanted!" He showed off his new skates and asked Uncle Luke to take him skating out at Granny's. When Uncle Luke and Daddy said the skating would have to wait, Chesler grabbed his new rod and reel. Daddy just nodded and said, "When the snow melts, Chesler."

So he plugged in the cassette player and started singing Christmas songs at the top of his lungs. I liked watching Chesler be so happy, and I think Daddy did too. As I listened to Chesler sing "Joy to the World," I rubbed my thumb over the matchbook in my pocket.

"So, Chesler, is there anything under the tree Santa might have left for your sister?"

Chesler looked around and picked up a square box. "This is for you, Kate. It's wrapped real pretty." He handed it to me.

I untied the large green ribbon and lifted the lid. My camera. My very own camera.

"And here's something else, Kate. No, it's two things." Chesler lugged over a heavy-looking box and put it on the floor in front of me. Then he put a smaller one on top.

I opened the smaller one first. "A package of water-color paper."

Uncle Luke laughed. "Santa Claus must have gotten confused. You can't put watercolor paper in a camera. You need film."

"Surely Santa wouldn't get confused about something like that. Maybe you should open the big one, Kate." Daddy pushed the large box toward me.

I opened it. On the front was a picture of a drawing table.

Uncle Luke came over to look. "Wow, Kate. You can open your own art studio now. Watercolor paper and a drawing table and a camera." Uncle Luke picked up my camera. "Look. It's already got the batteries and film in it. Santa thought of everything. Guess all you have to do now is point and shoot."

I just smiled at Daddy. "Great! Daddy, you and Uncle Luke and Chesler, go sit in front of the Christmas tree. This will be my very first picture." Daddy and Uncle Luke sat on the floor shoulder to shoulder, and Chesler sat on their shoulders right between them. "Smile big, you guys." I snapped the picture.

"Looks like that's all from Santa, but there'll be lots more presents when Granny Grace and Aunt Susannah Hope and Uncle Don get here. What time is it?"

Chesler ran to the front hall to look at the grandfather clock. "It's three after seven." We knew that meant seven fifteen. That was just Chesler's way of telling time.

"We'd better get going. Granny'll be coming in that door about eight o'clock. Luke, you going to get Lisa?"

"I'll call her and pick her up as soon as she's ready."

"Well, let's get up those stairs and get ready for the day."

"Wait, a few more pictures. Uncle Luke, you and Chesler roll around in the Christmas paper." I knew Chesler would like that and I wouldn't have to tell him to smile. I liked having that camera hanging around my neck and clicking the button on top.

After I finished, Uncle Luke said, "Okay, upstairs, you two."

I took a shower, dried my hair, and got dressed. I was putting a ribbon around my ponytail when Chesler came running into my room. "Kate, are you sure you're not mad at me for telling Daddy where you were?"

I tightened the bow around my hair. "I already told you no, Chesler. I'm not mad at you. I'd still be in the church all alone if you hadn't told him. So I'm not mad."

"I'm sorry you got stuck at church, but I know you weren't alone because Mama's present was gone this morning." That was the smartest thing my little brother ever said.

Daddy was in the kitchen when Granny and my aunt and uncle arrived. The Christmas mugs were already on the counter. I would use Mama's this year, and I'd give mine to Aunt Lisa. Mama made it our family tradition to drink hot chocolate with homemade cinnamon rolls on Christmas morning. Then we would drink our second cup of hot chocolate around the tree while Grandpa read the real Christmas story. Mama and Grandpa weren't here this year, but Daddy remembered and made a big pot of real hot chocolate like Mama would have made.

Granny Grace was taking the foil off her warm cinnamon rolls when Uncle Luke and Aunt Lisa walked in. "Merry Christmas, you two. Lisa, we couldn't be happier to have you in this family."

I kept clicking the button on my new camera, taking pictures of happy faces when they weren't looking.

Aunt Susannah Hope handed out Christmas plates with hot cinnamon rolls, and Daddy gave everybody a mug of hot chocolate. When we all had a cup, Granny lifted hers high. "Merry Christmas, everybody. Eat your breakfast. This is it because we're having a lunch the likes of which you haven't seen since last Christmas."

We sat around the table in the kitchen and ate our cinnamon rolls. Everybody was talking, but nobody said a word about last night and my getting locked in the church. I think Uncle Luke told Aunt Lisa, though, because she just looked like she knew something, but she wouldn't say it.

Granny Grace passed the plate of rolls around again. "Well, for little old ladies like me and for young boys like Chesler and for everybody in between, it's real important to carry on traditions. And that's what we're about to do, so get yourself another cup of hot chocolate and let's go to the living room." Granny was in charge again, and we followed her orders.

Uncle Don sat in his favorite spot on the sofa, and Aunt Susannah Hope curled up beside him. Uncle Luke pulled up the straight chair and sat next to the Christmas tree. Aunt Lisa and Chesler and I sat at his feet. We knew that Granny and Daddy would be sitting in the chairs on each side of the fireplace. Daddy held his Bible in his lap, and everybody was talking happy talk, and then Aunt Susannah spoke up.

"I need to tell you all something."

Everybody hushed. I looked at Daddy, and he had that look like he always has when there's trouble.

Aunt Susannah Hope looked back at Uncle Don. Her lips almost smiled, but she looked more like she was about to cry. "I know I've not been the easiest person to get along with lately, and I know you have been a little worried about me. And Luke, I want to thank you for insisting that I go to the doctor and have some tests."

Nobody in the room wanted to hear what we thought she was gonna say.

"The doctor says there is absolutely nothing wrong with me."

Granny looked the most relieved. "Thank God for that, Susannah."

Aunt Susannah kept talking. "But what he did say is there is something absolutely right with me. When we gather here next Christmas, there will be a new family member along with Lisa." She paused. "We're having a baby."

There was more noise and more hugging going on in that room than when Chesler was opening his presents.

Granny was so happy. "Well, I'd say that's about the best Christmas present ever. A baby for next Christmas! Fancy that."

When everybody sat back down, I felt all quiet inside and just looked around the room. Home hadn't looked so good since Mama went to heaven, but it looked good to me this morning. It didn't have anything to do with all the presents under the tree or my new camera. But it felt warm like it had a blanket around it, and it smelled like home. I missed Mama at the tree. I missed her singing. And I'd bet Mama would be so happy about the baby she'd still be hugging Aunt Susannah Hope.

Daddy opened up his Bible and started to read from the Book of Luke just like Grandpa used to do. While he was reading, I wondered if they had Christmas trees and presents in heaven, and if Mama and Grandpa were sitting around a great big tree like we were this morning. When Daddy finished reading, Uncle Don prayed. I took one more picture with everybody's eyes closed. I wanted to remember this.

It was time for presents. Daddy said, "Chesler, now that you can read a little bit, it's going to be your first Christmas to hand out the presents. Can you do that?"

"Yes, sir." Chesler shouted each name real loud like they wouldn't know it was their present if he didn't. He hurried to pass them out so he could start opening the boxes with his name on them.

Christmas wrappings started flying again, and Aunt Susannah Hope was off the sofa and grabbing the Christmas paper as it flew and gathering it up off the floor, but Daddy stopped her. I knew why. Mama liked to see the room covered in paper.

Aunt Lisa did what she promised. She framed and wrapped the sketches of Mama I made for Granny and my aunt. They both had a good cry when they saw the pictures I drew.

Daddy bragged on the fish tray I made him just like Aunt Lisa said he would. Everybody had their laps full of boxes, and the floor was knee-deep in Christmas paper, just like Mama would like it. No more gifts under the tree, and I thought it was time to get ready for church, but Aunt Susannah Hope pulled out two more huge presents from somewhere. Everybody got real quiet again.

She handed one to Chesler and one to me. Her voice sounded like she was going to cry, and I didn't want to look at her. "This is something your mama wanted you to have. She started it before she went to heaven, and Granny Grace and I finished it so you could have it for Christmas."

Chesler tore into his box like somebody might take it away him, but I opened mine real careful like, not ripping the tissue. Chesler spread his out all over the floor before I could pull out my very own patchwork quilt. There were pieces of Mama's pink dress and her favorite blouse with the roses and pieces of my clothes I had outgrown. Granny Grace said it was a memory quilt of Mama's things and some of our own clothes, even our christening gowns, and they were all stitched together with love just like we were. I held it to my face. It smelled like Mama.

Granny Grace said, "Look in the bottom of the box, Katy. Your mama wanted you to have this too."

There was a small, pink satin bag with a white ribbon drawstring and a card. I opened the bag first. It was a lock of Mama's red hair tied with more white ribbon. My heart stopped. Mama and I had thought of the exact same Christmas present! I was thinking like Mama, just like Mr. Josh said I would when I grew up. Now a part of Mama would be with me forever too.

The card was in Mama's curlicue handwriting.

My sweet Kate, my Katherine Joy,

It's our first Christmas apart. These gifts are to remind you that I'm always as close as your thoughts of me. This quilt will wrap you in warm memories and my nearness. You were created and born in love, and you'll forever be my daughter. Be happy, Kate. Be kind to others and be good to yourself. And, Katherine Joy, you be aware of all the wonders that others miss, especially the redbird. I love you. And remember always, faith, family, and forever.

Merry Christmas,
Mama

I put the card and the lock of Mama's hair back in the bag and ran my hand over the quilt. Then I saw the redbird, the one she had stitched by hand with silk thread on a large white square right in the middle. Mama thought of everything. Christmas didn't go to heaven when she did.

Before we left for church, I went upstairs and spread my quilt on top of my bed. From now on Mama would be all around me. The matchbook I found in my pocket this morning, the one with Haven of Hope on it, was lying on my desk. I took the pink satin bag with Mama's lock of hair in it and opened it. The perfect place for my new treasures. I stuck the matchbook right next to Mama's curl and pulled the drawstring shut and put the bag under my pillow.

Christmas was different now that Mama and Grandpa were in heaven, but today was a good day. After we read the Christmas story and opened our presents, we all scrunched up and drove to church together in Uncle Don's van, with Chesler singing at the top of his lungs,

"All Is Well." I liked it that Christmas this year came on a Sunday. It just fit the day somehow.

Laramie and her mom and dad met us at church and sat with our family on the third pew. She and her mom held hands the whole time. So did Uncle Luke and Aunt Lisa.

Daddy sat between Chesler and me, and Granny sat next to Aunt Susannah Hope and patted her leg about fifty times.

Miss Evie was there too. I got to tell her about my new camera. She said she wanted to come see it.

It was hard to listen to Pastor Simmons because all I could think about was last night and being locked in the church. But the best part was giving Mama her present and getting a lock of hair in that silk bag.

Laramie and her parents followed us home after the service. Granny was right about the lunch. It was the most food we'd seen on that old dining room table since Thanksgiving. The only thing was Aunt Susannah Hope had to run down the hall when Granny told her there were oysters in the dressing. Granny said she'd be like that for a few more weeks, then she would feel better than she'd ever felt in her life until the baby came.

After all the eating and laughing and storytelling, everybody went home. The house was quiet again, but a different kind of quiet—like Mama used to like. The kind of quiet that says it's been a good day and all is well.

I guess Mama was right when she told me life goes on, like the stream always heading somewhere. Sure seemed that way. Uncle Luke was getting married. My aunt was having a baby when she didn't think she could. Laramie was my new best friend. Chesler was growing up a little bit at a time, and Daddy was settling in to taking care of me and Chesler without Mama's help.

And me, I was growing up too. I'd be taking my own pictures and making my own Books of My Life from now on and Chesler's too, just like Mama wanted me to.

I dressed for bed and hung up my Christmas clothes. Tonight would be my first night under the quilt Mama made me. I went to sleep with my pink satin bag in my hand.

The next morning Daddy made good on his promise to take my first roll of film to the one-hour photo counter at the drugstore. We hung around the store, buying a few things on Christmas clearance and waiting for the photos. Then we picked up Laramie. She was going to stay with us so her mom and dad could have some time to talk.

When we finally got back home, I practically dragged Laramie up the stairs to my room 'cause I couldn't wait to tell her how my plan worked. I threw the packet of photos on my bed and said, "I have to show you something." She picked up the envelope of photos while I fished under my pillow for my treasure bag. I told her everything that happened and showed her the green matchbook.

"I believed you even without the matches." Laramie sat on the bed and opened the envelope and looked at the first picture.

I was just about to say something when she jerked her head around, her eyes beaming. She looked straight at me and smiled just like she did when her mom walked through the front door on Christmas Eve.

"What is it, Laramie?" She handed the photo to me. "Here, Kate, you're not going to believe this." Then she smiled.

My first photograph. There they were—Daddy, Uncle Luke, and Chesler, sitting on the floor by the Christmas tree right by the window. And there I was, my own reflection in the mirror across the room, camera in front of my face.

"Do you see it? The redbird?"

I held the picture closer and stared at it. Then I saw it, the redbird with her head cocked just so and sitting on the window ledge looking in just like she belonged there.

Laramie was right—I couldn't believe it. I was in my very first photograph, and so was the redbird. A real family Christmas portrait.

EPILOGUE

Chicago
December 2006

*W*HILE WE WAITED on her mother, Marla sat on the sofa in the foyer of my office and finished telling me about her conversation with Mr. Josh. "Why does he have all those colors on him?" She pointed back to the picture.

"Because that's the way I like to think about him."

"He looks like he got caught in a rainbow."

I chuckled. "Perhaps he did."

"But it's dark all around him. How can you have a rainbow in the dark?"

"Marla, you ask the best questions."

The clanging bell indicated someone had opened the front door. Marla turned to see. "It's Mama." She jumped up and ran toward the door. "Bye, Dr. Kate. See you next year. Oh, and merry Christmas."

She was halfway out the door to meet her mother when I managed a "Merry Christmas to you too, Marla." I watched Marla hug her mother. Silhouetted against the late December afternoon sky dotted with Christmas lights, they walked hand in hand across the street to their car.

I turned to the quilt hanging on the wall behind me and ran my fingers over the silk thread outlining the redbird. Then I glanced at the Christmas photo hanging next to the quilt—my first photograph, the one I took on that first Christmas morning after Mama went to heaven. I pondered that day for a few more moments before locking the door and turning out the front lights. I'd be in Cedar Falls this time tomorrow afternoon, joining my family for Christmas again.

Eighteen years had passed since that first Christmas portrait. Life changed when Mama died, and sometimes, I wondered how things might have been if she were still with us. She left too soon, but she left us with so much.

Granny Grace loved every day at her farm, continued singing in the choir, chased more guineas, and passed out orders to all the family until age eighty-four. She went to sleep one April evening and woke up in her heavenly mansion, built with only God knows how many blueberry pies and Japanese fruitcakes and other acts of kindness.

Aunt Susannah Hope and Uncle Don still live in the white Victorian with the wrap-around porch and picket fence. Somehow my aunt's attacks of breathlessness went away after she had two children. Uncle Don still runs his accounting business when he isn't painting windowsills or following up on Aunt Susannah Hope's honey-do list. Hank, their first, is a college freshman studying architecture, and Gracie is still in high school. Gracie has Mama's red hair.

Uncle Luke and Aunt Lisa married, and he set up his family practice in Cedar Falls. They bought Granny's farm and added practically another house onto that log cabin. And now their three children fish in the pond where Uncle Luke proposed to Aunt Lisa.

Chesler. He is in school to be a veterinarian. He spent the last three summers working on a dude ranch in Colorado and singing tenor with a cowboy quartet for nightly entertainment at the chuckwagon dinners. Daddy said Chesler was going to be a singing cowboy vet.

And Daddy. Well, Daddy became Uncle Luke's physician's assistant, and he is still taking care of people. Evie, Pastor Simmons's sister, moved to Cedar Falls shortly after the Christmas we met her and set up her studio and gallery there. It was small but successful. Two years later Daddy married Evie. I was the twelve-year-old maid of honor at their wedding and Chesler sang. Evie taught me so much about cameras and how to see things, really see things, and she made Daddy happy again. I still take trips with them a couple times a year. Daddy follows us to all kinds of exotic places and carries our camera equipment. Evie and I are collaborating on a book, a coffee table collection of happy faces from around the world. Mama would be proud.

Laramie and I are still friends. Although we don't get to see each other as much as we'd like, we chat often. She and her parents moved back East to be with her grandparents when Laramie was fifteen, so we didn't graduate together, but she's done well. She's married, lives in Richmond, Virginia, and is the buyer of women's fashions for a large department store chain. She will meet me in Cedar Falls in June for the wedding.

And me? Well, little Kate now hangs out her shingle as Dr. Katherine Joy Harding, a licensed counselor and art therapist in Chicago. I still have the first camera I got for Christmas the year Mama went to heaven, and I am working on the next book of my life. Daddy, Chesler, and Uncle Luke are relieved that I'll become Mrs. Henry Beckenworth this summer. Henry's a social worker I met at a conference two years ago, and one day we'd like to go back to Appalachia, near my family, and do our work there. I wear his grandmother's engagement ring on my finger, a family heirloom and my newest treasure.

I still value the old treasures though, like my box of Christmas ornaments, and the note Mama wrote to her fifth-grade boyfriend, which is now stuck with chewing gum to the bottom of my office desk drawer, and the pink satin bag with the lock of Mama's hair and the mysterious Haven of Hope matchbook. I try to do the things Mama taught me—to be kind to others, kind enough to make them smile. I try to be good to myself and aware of the wonders that others miss.

Most of my practice involves grieving children, and it seems that Mr. Josh, the mysterious one who comes when children need him most, is still moving around just like he told me he does. I find myself looking for him, and I think I might have caught a couple glimpses of him since that Christmas of my tenth year, but the children who come to me often tell me of their conversations with him. He doesn't always tell them his name, perhaps because they don't ask. Oh, he dresses differently, and most children don't see him the way I painted him in a rainbow of colors, but his caring eyes and his gentle words are still the same. He shows up at parks, in hospitals, in churches, and all kinds of surprising places. One of these days I'll have my camera ready.

And Mama? Like Mr. Josh said, I hear her in my voice sometimes, and I see a bit of her when I look in the mirror. She still feels near, and there always seems to be a redbird close by.

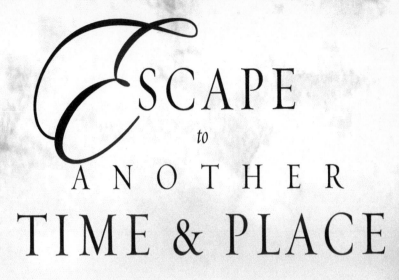

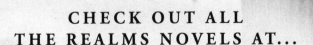

Be Empowered
Be Encouraged
Be Inspired
Be SpiritLed
FREE NEWSLETTERS
Empowering Women for Life in the Spirit
SPIRITLED WOMAN
Amazing stories, testimonies, and articles on marriage, family, prayer, and more.
POWER UP! FOR WOMEN
Receive encouraging teachings that will empower you for a Spirit-filled life.
CHARISMA MAGAZINE
Get top-trending articles, Christian teachings, entertainment reviews, videos, and more.
CHARISMA NEWS DAILY
Get the latest breaking news from an evangelical perspective. Sent Monday-Friday.
SIGN UP AT: nl.charismamag.com
CHARISMA MEDIA
P0780